NO QUESTIONS ASKED
OLIVER BLEECK

"A great deal of action in a well-developed plot makes [this] a successful and exciting novel.... Bleeck's style is polished and vivid."

—*Best Sellers*

"Well-written, neat and effective."

—*The Times Literary Supplement*

NO QUESTIONS ASKED

OLIVER BLEECK

PERENNIAL LIBRARY
Harper & Row, Publishers
New York, Cambridge, Philadelphia, San Francisco
London, Mexico City, São Paulo, Singapore, Sydney

First PERENNIAL LIBRARY edition published 1984.

Library of Congress Cataloging in Publication Data

Bleeck, Oliver, 1926-
  No questions asked.

  "Perennial Library."
  I. Title.
[PS3570.H58N6 1984]   813'.54   83-48947
ISBN 0-06-080703-2 (pbk.)

84 85 86 87 88 10 9 8 7 6 5 4 3 2 1

NO
QUESTIONS
ASKED

ONE

The only thing in the mail that day of any interest was the eviction notice. There was also a letter from *The Wall Street Journal*, which promised that I could get fairly rich if only I would subscribe for just six months, while down in Atlanta Julian Bond had written, wanting to know whether I wouldn't like to send along another $25 to help keep the Republic fairly honest.

I tossed *The Wall Street Journal*'s promise into the wastebasket, made a mental note to cut Julian Bond off with $10, and handed the eviction notice to Myron Greene, the lawyer, who had brought my mail up with him that morning.

Myron Greene read the letter slowly and suspiciously, the way lawyers read everything, even the close-cover-before-striking admonition on match folders. He read it once at arm's length, then put on a pair of grey-tinted aviator glasses, and read it again. After that he shrugged and handed it back to me.

"It's an eviction notice," he said.

"I know what it is," I said. "What I don't know is what I can do about it."

Myron Greene glanced around the room and although he must have tried, he couldn't keep the small expression of disapproval from sliding across his face. He shook his head and said, "There's really only one thing you can do about it."

"What?"

"Move."

I looked around trying to see it through the eyes of some benevolent Christian whom the Goodwill people had sent over and who was viewing it all for the first time. What I was being evicted from was a "deluxe" efficiency on the ninth floor of the Adelphi apartment hotel on East Forty-sixth Street. It was about 425 square feet of steam-heated space that contained virtually everything I owned in the world other than the $9,215.26 in a checking account over which the Chase Manhattan Bank was standing constant vigil.

I decided that even a benevolent Goodwill representative, who had shaped his career out of cheerfully collecting other people's discards, might have gulped and sighed before agreeing to accept mine. There was a book-lined wall, but most of the books were worn paperbacks except for a leatherbound set of Dickens, although nobody reads Dickens much anymore. The bed was what I think they used to call a studio couch and it was beginning to sag a bit. There was also a leather wingbacked easy chair that I liked a lot and a small Sony color TV set whose predominantly yellowish cast made everyone, especially Sevareid, appear faintly choleric.

Then in front of the Pullman kitchen was the 121-year-old butcher block that I pounded the round steak on. Not far from it against the wall was the high-fidelity set that played just fine even though after I had put it all together there had been a couple of loose wires left over.

On the floor was a rug and on the walls were some prints that I still didn't mind looking at and in the center of the room, surrounded by six mismatched, straightbacked chairs, was where I took my meals and sometimes laid my money down. It was a hexagonal poker table whose green baize cover was marred by a dark stain that had been caused when a Homicide South detective had got all excited after filling an inside straight and knocked over his Bloody Mary at 5:15 one Sunday morning.

Myron Greene and I were sitting at the poker table, he in his dark blue pin-striped vested suit and I in my terry-cloth bathrobe.

"You have to be in court today, don't you?" I said.

"How do you know?"

"You're either going to court or to a funeral. Otherwise you'd be wearing something more dashing. Maybe something in crushed velvet with a few posies appliquéd on the back." Myron Greene liked to think of himself as a dandy, but he wasn't too sure about his taste, and he liked me to encourage him.

He glanced down at his suit and brushed away some imaginary lint. "It's five years old and it still fits perfectly."

"You haven't lost any weight in five years."

"You can be awfully snotty in the morning."

"I'm always snotty when I get up in the morning without any coffee and somebody hands me an eviction notice. You want some coffee?"

"Is it instant?"

"It's always instant."

Myron Greene shook his head. "Then I don't want any."

"How about some tea?" I said.

Myron Greene had to think about that because it was a decision, and he never made decisions without weighing the consequences carefully and even judiciously. His inbred caution, along with his brilliant grasp of the law, kept his corporate clients out of trouble and had made him wealthy, if not really rich, although he probably would be that in a few more years.

"All right," he said. "Tea. No sugar. Lemon, if you've got it."

"I've got it."

I went over to the kitchen, filled the kettle, and put it on to heat. Then I turned, lost another battle with my willpower, and lit a cigarette. This time Myron Greene didn't try to hide his disapproval.

"You shouldn't smoke before you've had breakfast," he said.

"I shouldn't smoke at all."

"Then why don't you quit? It's not all that hard. I did it."

8

"You quit five cigarettes a day, tops, and when you did you put on twenty pounds. I think I'll stay svelte and cough a lot."

Myron Greene sighed. He seemed to sigh often and deeply when he was around me. He sighed over my profligate ways, my slothful nature, and the company I kept. He sighed because I wasn't more like him and then sighed again over the realization that if I were more like him, I wouldn't be his client, and he would have lost his only contact with somebody who inhabited what he thought of as a netherworld peopled by latter-day Robin Hoods and their merrymen who raced through life, knew a lot of blondes, and scoffed at their parking tickets because they knew how to get them fixed. If it weren't for the wife and kids and the money, especially the money, Myron Greene would have liked to have been a slick criminal lawyer who wore flashy clothes and got his name in the paper all the time.

Instead, he settled for clients who had made him a millionaire before he was forty, which enabled him to live in Darien, maintain a summer home in Kennebunkport, drive a $20,000 Mercedes 450 SCL, and keep me on as a client. But I don't think I was really ever a client of Myron Greene's. I think I was his hobby.

I set the teapot and a cup and saucer in front of him, went back and got my coffee and the lemon, and sat back down at the poker table. He poured his tea, squeezed the lemon into it, tasted it, and smiled.

"It's good," he said.

"It's Twinings Irish breakfast tea. It's got a nip to it."

"Why do you always go to the trouble of making a

real pot of tea, but when it comes to coffee you drink that awful instant stuff?"

I shrugged. "I don't know. I suppose it's because of that time when I lived in England."

"When you were with the paper."

"Yeah. When I was with the paper."

"That must have been ten years ago now."

"More like twelve or thirteen."

I had once written a thrice-weekly column for one of those New York papers that had gone out of business in the mid-sixties. I had written mostly about the quaint ways of New York's mountebanks and hustlers and con artists and of cops who were honest and brave and of those who were only partly so. Just before the paper folded there had been some talk of syndication, but nothing ever came of it, and largely through chance I found myself doing what I now do for a living, which is mostly waiting for Myron Greene to come calling.

He finished his cup of tea, used his breast pocket handkerchief to pat his lips, since I hadn't thought to provide napkins, put it back carefully just the way it was, and pursed his lips now that they were dry in a thoughtful way, which meant that he felt that he had something important and even grave to say.

"I received three calls this morning," he said. "Quite early this morning. Before seven."

"That's pretty early," I said.

"I tentatively agreed for you to handle it although, of course, I said that I would have to check with you first."

"How much?" I said.

10

"A quarter of a million."

"My end's the usual ten percent?"

Myron Greene nodded.

"Who's going to pay it?"

"The insurance company has agreed to pay it, if you can get it back."

"Then it must be worth a lot more than a quarter of a million, whatever it is, which you're going to tell me about in due course, although at this rate due course is probably going to be late this afternoon."

Myron Greene sighed again. It must have been either his third or fourth sigh, but I was no longer counting. "If you don't mind, I'd like to present it in my own way. My own way is a logical, step-by-step presentation, which, I realize, is a bit foreign to you."

"Don't try to be sarcastic, Myron. When you try to be sarcastic you get all red in the face. You want some more tea?"

Myron Greene started to touch his face to see whether it was red, but realized what he was doing and stroked his moustache instead. The moustache was new. At least I hadn't seen it before and I knew he was waiting for me to say something about it and I was trying very hard not to. We played little games like that with each other.

"I would like some more tea," he said. "The first call I got was from the insurance company."

"Have we done any business with them before?" I said as I poured.

He shook his head and gave his moustache another brush with a thumbnail. Actually, I thought the moustache made him look rather dashing, if somebody who stands five nine and weighs close to a hundred and ninety-five pounds can look dashing.

"It's a Los Angeles firm," he said. "It's comparatively small, but growing, and they've established quite a sound reputation for themselves despite the fact that they occasionally do some rather odd business."

"How odd?"

"They insure such things as movie actresses' legs and smiles and tits and things like that. But the firm's sound. Very sound. I suppose they do it for the publicity."

"What have they insured that we're interested in?"

"A book."

"A book? Just one?"

Myron Greene nodded. "That's right. Just one. Now the second call I received this morning, again quite early, I might add, was from Washington."

"Ah," I said.

"What does 'ah' mean?"

"I don't know," I said. "I suppose it means that the plot thickens. That's what a call from Washington can mean, especially if it's from the CIA or the State Department or somebody jazzy like that."

"It was from the Library of Congress."

"Well, that's where they keep books. In fact, they keep some pretty valuable ones there."

"Valuable and rare. The call was from the Chief of the Rare Book Division."

"He's missing a rare book, I take it."

Myron Greene shook his head. "No, that was the principal reason he called. He wanted to make it quite clear that the book in question had only been on deposit with the Library and that the owner had insisted on withdrawing it, using his own security measures and not those of the Library or of the federal government for that matter."

"So somebody stole it after it left the Library?"

"Apparently so. However, the man I talked to, a Mr. Laws, while insisting that neither the Library nor the government had any responsibility for the book's theft, also wanted me to know that they would cooperate in any way that they could in securing its retrieval."

"You mean getting it back."

"That's what I said."

I shook my head. "You said securing its retrieval. Five minutes on the phone with Washington and you start talking the way they do down there."

"It must be contagious," he said. "Now then. The third call. It must have been long distance, too, but I'm not absolutely sure. It had that funny kind of hum that long distance has. It was from a woman or a man who was trying to sound like a woman who was trying to disguise her voice."

"Tricky," I said. "And also a new wrinkle. Nobody's ever used that one on me before. What did he or she want?"

"We'll make it she. She said that you had been recommended by the insurance company, but she didn't know anything about you. She wanted to know somebody she could talk to about you who was in her line of work."

"What's her line of work?"

"She said she was a thief."

"What did you say?"

"I said that most of the people whom you knew who were in her line of work were in jail—although through no fault of yours. Then I thought of somebody."

"Who?"

"Bingo Bobby."

"Good Lord," I said. "Bingo Bobby Bishop. I haven't thought of him in years. I also thought he was doing ten to twenty down in Oklahoma. McAlester, wasn't it?"

"It was," Myron Greene said, "but he got out. He called me about a month ago and wanted to know if I could recommend some young, really smart lawyer who was just starting out in practice and didn't charge too much."

"For himself?"

"He said for a friend. I took his number and then called him back and gave him the name of a kid I know who'd just got out of law school. He thanked me and told me to tell you hello. So I gave his number to the woman."

"The one who called you this morning. Well, if she wanted to talk to a thief, he's a good one."

Myron Greene sipped his tea. "He must have given you a good reference because she called me back."

"The thief?"

"Yes."

"What'd she say?"

"She said she thought she'd be able to work with you. I told her that I would have to talk with you first, but that I felt sure that you'd be interested. You are interested, aren't you?"

"I'm interested."

"Then you have to be in Washington this evening to meet with the insurance company's representative who's flying in from Los Angeles. He and the Chief of the Rare Book Division will brief you on the book."

"You mean they might even mention its name."

"I didn't forget to mention it, if that's what you mean. They wouldn't tell me. All they would say is that it's old and rare and extremely valuable."

"How old?"

"A little less than five hundred years old, they said. Oh, yes. The thief wanted to know one more thing. She wanted to know what to call you. I said she could call you Mr. St. Ives or Philip or even Phil, if you grew really chummy. She said she didn't mean your name, she meant what you did for a living. I told her that she could think of you as a professional intermediary."

"You shouldn't try to pretty it up," I said. "Professional intermediary is what you put down on my tax returns. You should have told her what I really am since she says she's a thief, which almost makes her part of the family."

"You mean go-between?"

"That's right, Myron. Go-between."

―――――――――――――――――― TWO

The Adelphi apartment hotel that they were going
to tear down and evict me from, although not in that
order, had been built back in the early twenties about
the time that the claw-footed bathtub was beginning to
disappear from the American scene.

Because a long series of owners had refused to spend
what they should have on maintenance, the Adelphi
had skipped middle age and instead had gone directly
into advanced senility. The heating system wheezed and
drooled. The elevators were spiteful, the way a mean
old lady can be spiteful, and kept letting you off on the
wrong floor. The walls were cracked and stained and a
musty grey, although they once must have been an
oyster white. The carpets were worn and patched, and
you kept tripping over them. The bar and restaurant
off the lobby was patronized largely by utter strangers
who tried it only once by dreadful accident. And then
there was Eddie, the sinister bell captain.

Eddie was one of those persons who make a lot of

16

tourists loathe New York. His was the elbow that dug into them in the subway. His back was what they saw getting into the taxi that they knew was theirs. And his was the voice that promised them twenty-year-old blondes, but delivered forty-five-year-old hookers instead.

After ten years of diligent effort Eddie had almost given up trying to hustle me. But not quite. I think he thought of me as a worthy opponent who put him on his mettle. If you wanted a service performed such as having your dog walked or somebody's arm broken, Eddie would do it or get it done. If you needed a broad, booze, dope, or a desert lot, Eddie would sell it to you. For a price he would lie to your boss, stall the collection agency, or even get you a cab, which is what I had in mind when I got off the elevator carrying my suitcase.

"I want a four-bit cab," I told him as he took my bag.

"Whaddaya mean four bits? That's all you ever tip."

"And that's the kind of cab you always hail. You know, the kind with the broken shocks, the ripped upholstery, and the driver who speaks nothing but Kurdish."

"We like to kid a little this morning, don't we? Where to?"

"La Guardia. Eastern shuttle."

"Washington, huh? You always get in trouble when you go to Washington."

"Not always. I didn't get in trouble that time I took my son down to see the cherry blossoms."

"How is he? I ain't seen him in a while."

"He's okay."

17

"What is he now, ten?"

"Yeah. Ten."

"You know what I hear? I hear his new daddy took a real bath in the market. That's what I hear."

"I've sort of been worrying about that," I said. "He must be down to his last thirty or forty million."

We were outside on Forty-sixth by now and Eddie was using his fingers to whistle up a cab, but I could see that his heart wasn't in it yet.

"Your ex really done all right for herself, didn't she, I mean by leaving you and marrying what's his face with all that dough?"

"I don't know," I said. "He probably doesn't pick up his pajamas either."

Eddie gave another whistle through his fingers and then turned to me with his usual sly and crafty look. "I sent the eviction letter up with your lawyer this morning."

"I forgot to thank you for it, didn't I? How long have you known, six months?"

"Nah. Just a couple of months. Maybe three."

"You can certainly keep a secret, Eddie."

"I tipped off a couple of people. Y'know, the ones who've took care of me good."

"Well, I've tried not to fail you. I've tried terribly hard."

"Yeah, shit. Well, these people I tipped off. I sort of helped them find a new place, y'know?"

"You're not only generous, you're sweet."

"Yeah, well, I thought maybe you'd want me to sort of help you out. I know a place that'd just suit you down to a T. Over on West Fifty-sixth. Hell of a nice

18

place. One bedroom, big living room, air-conditioned."

"How much?"

"Not bad. Not bad at all. Six twenty-five a month."

"I don't mean how much for the rent. I mean how much for the key?"

Eddie shrugged, spotted a cab, and gave another blast through his fingers. The cab started nudging its way through the traffic toward the curb. "Well, you know how these things work," he said. "You gotta grease a few palms."

"How much key money, Eddie?"

"Seeing how it's you, only three grand."

"Forget it."

"Think it over," he said as he put my bag in the front seat and turned with his hand out. I put two quarters into it.

"I don't have to think it over," I said. "But just out of curiosity, who owns the building, your brother-in-law?"

"Nah," Eddie said and smiled. "I do."

To the best of my knowledge nobody has ever written a song entitled "April in Washington," and it's not hard to understand why. It was April 15, a little after one in the afternoon, when I arrived at National Airport and took a cab to the Hay Adams hotel. It was a warm, even balmy, day, and scores of government workers were still picnicking out of their brown bag lunches in Lafayette Square.

When I came out of the hotel two hours later the temperature had dropped twenty-five degrees, it was threatening to spit snow, and the talkative cab driver I got told me that they were thinking of closing the government offices early.

"They're just thinking about it though," he said. "By the time they make up their mind it'll be five o'clock and there'll be six inches of snow on the ground."

"Is that what the weather forecast says?"

"Nah. That's what I say. We didn't used to have weather like this in this town. Only in the past two or three years. Before that we used to have pretty good weather. You know what I think caused it?"

"What?"

"Watergate."

"That's a thought."

"Way I figure it, Watergate got people all steamed up, I mean it really affected the temperature of their bodies, and all this steam had to go some place, so it went up and made clouds and so that's why we got a lot more rain and snow now than we used to."

We were going east on Pennsylvania Avenue, and a new building that I hadn't seen before appeared on the left. It seemed to cover an entire block. "What's that?" I asked.

"That there?" the driver said. "That there's the new FBI building. Guess who they named it after?"

"Bobby Kennedy."

"Nah. J. Edgar Hoover. You know what he really was, don'tcha?"

"No. What?"

"He was the biggest fag in town, that's what he was. Jack Kennedy found out about it, and that's why Hoover had him shot down there in Dallas."

"I'll be damned," I said.

The driver nodded gloomily. "You drive a cab in this town and keep your ears open, you learn a lot of things."

We reached the First Street Southeast entrance to the Library of Congress without any more bulletins from the driver. "I wonder what they really do in there?" he said, eyeing the old building with what seemed to be faint suspicion.

"I think they lend books," I said.

"You know what I hear they got in there?" he said. "I hear they got the world's biggest collection of dirty books, but they won't let nobody but Congressmen or government big shots check 'em out."

"What a pity," I said, handed him the fare, and started to get out of the cab.

"You wanna know something else?"

I turned back to look at him. He was staring up at the Library with a moody expression. "I bet I ain't read a book in twenty-five years."

"It hardly shows at all," I said, got out of the cab, and went in search of a Mr. Hawkins Gamble Laws III who was going to tell me all about a book that had been borrowed without permission and wouldn't be returned until somebody came up with a quarter of a million dollars.

I asked a couple of tweedy gentlemen with short beards and thoughtful expressions where I could find the Rare Book Division. One of them turned out to be from Paris, judging from his accent, while the other volunteered the information that he was from Italy, Bologna to be exact, and had been working at something interesting, which I didn't quite catch, in the Hebraic Section of the Orientalia Division for the last twenty-one years. We had a nice little chat about that, and then I went off on my own, armed with their directions, and got lost only twice, probably on purpose, because the Library of Congress is an interesting place to wander around in. I especially liked the main reading room with its high ceiling, hushed atmosphere, and dedicated scholars who were looking into things that I had the feeling that I would like to know about.

The Rare Book Division was on the second floor of the east wing of the building. I wandered into its reading room first through a pair of fine bronze doors that were worth a look. There were three panels on each door emblazoned with printers' names and devices, and I recognized the device of Fust and Schoeffer, a couple of printers who supposedly used to work with Johann Gutenberg, the man who started it all. I also recognized the printer's mark of William Morris, the man who founded the Kelmscott Press, not the talent agency, and who, probably more than anybody else, got the country interested in fine printing again back in the 1890s.

The reading room of the Rare Book Division turned out to be a peaceful place with twenty-foot ceilings and an air of determined concentration. There were a couple of rows of nicely lit tables with comfortable looking chairs occupied by perhaps a dozen persons who wore rapt expressions and didn't move their lips while they read.

The office that the government provided for the Chief of its Rare Book Division wasn't overwhelming.

There was a nice desk and some upholstered chairs and a few pictures, but there wasn't anything for show, and it could have been the office of the brigadier general out at the Pentagon who buys all of the Army's machine guns. Government offices tend to look pretty much alike.

But if you didn't remember the office, you remembered the man who occupied it. For one thing, Hawkins Gamble Laws III was probably one of the politest men I ever met in my life. After I was ushered in by his secretary, he shook my hand as if it were indeed the great pleasure he claimed it to be, saw to it that I got the room's most comfortable chair, dispatched his secretary for coffee, and then inquired solicitously about how he could best be of service. I got the feeling that if I had told him that I was down on my luck and needed a hundred until next Tuesday, he would have dug down into his own pocket and offered it without hesitation, except for the comment that if Tuesday didn't prove convenient, Friday would do just as well.

"The first thing you might tell me," I said, "is what was stolen from whom." I used whom because I thought that if I had said who it would have made him uncomfortable, although he would have been far too polite to have shown it. I noticed that he himself spoke a kind of mandarin English, touched up with plenty of commas and semicolons, which you don't run across too often in the United States unless you subscribe to *The Economist*.

"I really must apologize for not telling your attorney, Mr. Greene, the name of the book in question," Laws said. "However, when I explained my reasons he grasped the situation immediately, although it was an ungodly hour when circumstances forced me to telephone him."

"Myron's fairly quick in the morning," I said.

"He seemed a most perceptive chap. Sugar?"

"Please."

Instead of shoving the sugar bowl across the desk to me he rose, walked around, and held the bowl while I spooned what I needed into my cup. The sugar bowl looked to be silver as did the cream pitcher and the tray that they rested on. The cups were of a thin, translucent china, and I got the idea that when it came to personal possessions, Laws liked to have nice things around, although I noticed that his catalog of nice things didn't include a silver-frame portrait of the wife and kids. I decided that he must have felt his home life was a personal matter and not something that needed advertising.

Laws was somewhere in his late fifties, a tall man, really tall, but slightly stooped as if he were afraid that his height might make him miss something that he should be attentive and polite about. He wore a nicely cut grey flannel suit, the shade of old pewter, which went with his hair, and he was one of the few men I ever saw who didn't seem in the least self-conscious about the Phi Beta Kappa key that he wore on the gold chain across his vest.

He had a big, squarish head, almost too big, but not quite, and he kept cocking it to one side to show that he was both interested and attentive. His eyes were the twinkling kind, as brown and as friendly as a cocker pup's, and they didn't seem to need glasses, which I thought unusual. He smiled often and easily, as though he found the world a rather interesting, pleasant place to live in because it was populated with wonderful people like me, and after a few minutes in his beaming presence I had to forgive him for the fact that he parted his hair in the middle and wore a bow tie.

I sipped my coffee and complimented him on it, and he seemed genuinely pleased that I liked it. After that he gave his big chin a couple of reflective strokes, cocked his head to the other side as if to make sure that I was as comfortable as possible, hurriedly found an ashtray when I produced a cigarette, and leaned forward and lit it with a package of matches, which he insisted that I keep. I kept them, after first noting that they were from the Sans Souci, which is where all the important folks in Washington like to eat lunch.

"I take it then," he said, "that you have accepted the assignment to serve as intermediary in the return of the purloined book. Dear me, that must be the first time that I've used purloined in thirty years."

"You don't hear it much anymore," I said.

"We were, Mr. St. Ives, most distressed to learn that the book had been stolen, although our distress was somewhat alleviated by the fact that it was not stolen from the Library itself."

"So I understand."

"The book in question is quite old and quite rare and hence, quite valuable."

"How valuable?"

"That's difficult to say. On today's market, taking inflation into consideration, I should think that it would be snapped up at five hundred thousand dollars. It could bring as much as three-quarters of a million."

25

"It's not a Gutenberg Bible, is it?"

"Oh, dear me, no. I do believe we would have called out the National Guard if one of them had been stolen. We have three, you know."

"I didn't. Out of curiosity, what would one of them bring on today's market, if there is such a thing as a market for Gutenberg Bibles?"

Laws had to think about that. He gave his big chin another couple of reflective rubs, tugged at an earlobe, and took a sip of his coffee. "I would hesitate to say, but I think at least several million dollars. Back in 1930 the Library acquired Dr. Vollbehr's collection of three thousand incunabula, which at the time included one of the three known perfect copies on vellum of the Gutenberg Bible. It took a special Act of Congress, but we paid one and a half million dollars for the entire Vollbehr collection. However, Dr. Vollbehr himself had paid nearly three hundred and fifty thousand dollars for that particular Gutenberg, which made it at the time the highest price ever paid for a printed book. That, however, was nearly fifty years ago. Today?" Laws shrugged and let the question answer itself.

"The book that was stolen was what?"

"It was Pliny's *Historia Naturalis,*" Laws said. "Are you familiar with it?" He asked it politely, and when I shook my head no he smiled understandingly without any trace of condescension.

"No, I don't suppose too many people are nowadays, but it was the first scientific classic to be printed. Pliny the Elder, of course, was Gaius Plinius Secundus, the Roman naturalist, encyclopedist, and writer who lived from A.D. 23 to 79. The book was actually one of the chief repositories of scientific knowledge that scholars had available to them during the Middle Ages. This first edition that we're speaking of was one of the earliest books to be printed in Venice by Johaness de Spira."

"When was that?" I said.

"Prior to the eighteenth of September, 1469. Contemporary accounts reveal that only one hundred of the books were printed. Fortunately, the Library has another copy, which is part of the Rosenwald collection. But this particular volume, the one that was stolen, is the only one printed on vellum and is in much better condition than ours and, of course, is far, far more valuable. We were terribly upset by its theft."

"Tell me about it."

"The theft?"

"Yes."

"First, I should make it clear that the book was only on deposit with the Library. This means, in effect, that its owner had lent it to us with the understanding that we would use our own discretion in making it available to interested scholars. We were, I should add, awfully pleased to acquire it, even on a deposit basis. Last week, last Tuesday to be precise, the owner informed us that the book was to be withdrawn from deposit. We expressed our dismay, of course, but when the owner proved adamant, we offered to return the volume under special security arrangements."

"What kind of arrangements?" I said.

Laws took a sip of his coffee. "It depends upon the book, of course. But for one as valuable as the Pliny volume we would dispatch one of our senior staff members accompanied by an armed guard."

"But this didn't happen."

"No. The owner demurred and made other arrangements."

"Which were?"

"A private investigator, a Mr. Marsh, arrived yesterday morning and presented his credentials. We checked them carefully and turned the book over to him. Mr. Marsh has not been heard from since."

"What do the police say?"

"Quite frankly, Mr. St. Ives, I believe that the police are stumped. A Lt. Fastnaught is in charge of the investigation."

"Does he have curly blond hair and shiny blue eyes?"

"Why, yes, do you know him?"

"When I knew him he was only a sergeant, but he seemed ambitious. I guess it paid off. He hasn't got any leads, huh?"

"None, I'm afraid, but he hasn't exactly taken me into his confidence."

"The owner of the book?" I said.

"Yes?"

"Is he some kind of a nut?"

Laws smiled. It was a sad little smile which seemed to say that no, the owner wasn't a nut, just eccentric, more's the pity. "The owner is a she, Mr. St. Ives, a Miss or perhaps Ms. Maude Goodwater. Does the name Joiner Goodwater mean anything to you?"

"It rings a bell, but faintly," I said. "It has something to do with a lot of money that was made fast."

"Uranium," Laws said. "In the spring of 1947 Joiner Goodwater was a teacher of high-school science in Salt Lake City. That summer he went out into the Utah desert equipped with not much more than an army surplus Jeep, a canteen of water, a case or two of K rations, and a Geiger counter. When he came back in from the desert in late August he was an incredibly rich man."

"I remember," I said. "He found some of the richest uranium deposits in the country, and the paper started calling him the Uranium King. I also sort of remember that he spent it as fast as he made it."

"Not quite," Laws said. "But he seemed driven by the need to establish the Goodwater name as being among the principal art patrons of the country along with Guggenheim and Frick and Mellon and Rosenwald and even, I suppose," and here Laws sniffed a little, "Hirshhorn. Well, to make a sad story as brief as possible, he bought fine paintings by the yard and rare books by the case, but unfortunately the paintings that he bought were either not terribly good or masterful forgeries. He became, I regret to say, in art circles, at least, something of a laughingstock. Fortunately, he was more successful in the field of rare books. He concentrated on collecting rare scientific works and succeeded in putting together quite a nice little collection, the principal piece being, of course, the Pliny volume. It was placed upon deposit with us a little more than ten years ago with the tacit understanding that upon Mr. Goodwater's death it would become part of our permanent collection."

"He died, didn't he," I said. "About five years ago."

"Six," Laws said. "I think he died a broken, bitterly disappointed man. I knew him slightly, and he struck me as a man who—and I'm not being unkind—should have stayed in his high-school science laboratory. He was utterly unequipped for the business world in which he found himself."

"I remember reading about some of that," I said. "He got taken by every slick operator who came along."

"Not only that," Laws said, "but he began to have serious tax problems. What the slick operators, as you call them, didn't get, the tax people and the lawyers did, and when he died he was a relatively poor man."

"What's a relatively poor man?"

"Well, he had sold off his entire rare book collection, except for the Pliny volume. After the government collected what it said that he owed in taxes, I think his estate consisted of a house in Los Angeles, some terribly well-forged paintings, and perhaps a hundred thousand dollars or so in other assets."

"What did he go through—a couple of hundred million?"

"Something like that, I think."

"And now the Pliny book is about all that's left, except that it's been stolen."

"Yes."

"When the daughter, what's her name, Maude, decided to withdraw the Pliny volume from deposit, how did she go about it?"

Laws thought for a moment. "Her attorney in Los Angeles wrote to me on his letterhead advising me of her decision. I immediately got in touch with him by telephone, in an attempt to persuade him to help me change her mind."

"Did you ever talk to her?"

"Oh, yes. Several times. It really is a most remarkable

volume, and we were quite reluctant to see it leave the Library. Then, too, there was that tacit understanding that it would become part of the Library's permanent collection upon the death of Mr. Goodwater. Unfortunately, tacit agreements don't hold up too well in court, according to the Library's eminent legal counsel." Laws smiled faintly. "Of course, I'm not sure that we ever would have gone to court, although we can get rather tigerish when it comes to parting with a book as important as the Pliny."

"So you couldn't persuade the daughter?"

He shook his head. "She said that although she would very much like to leave it with the Library as a memorial to her father, she needed the money, and she had received a very generous offer for it, which she had decided to accept."

"Did she say whom the offer was from?"

"No, because she said the buyer insisted on remaining anonymous. However, she did tell me how much the offer was because I was hoping that if it were not too high the Library might have been able to match or perhaps even better it."

"But you weren't?"

Again Laws shook his head. "As I mentioned earlier, the Pliny would have been snapped up at five hundred thousand. Although I knew that we couldn't have come up with that amount out of our budget, I felt I could have gone to some private friends of the Library and possibly raised it from them, although money, as you know, is terribly tight these days."

"So how much was the offer that she got?"

Laws sighed. "Three-quarters of a million dollars."

I didn't whistle because I felt that Laws might feel that whistling was tacky. "Who has that kind of money?"

"Quite frankly, nobody," Laws said. "As you may suspect, Mr. St. Ives, we have an old-boy network in the rare book field, and I confess that I employed it in an attempt to find out who was making such an extraordinary offer for the Pliny. The consensus was that nobody was making such an offer, by that I mean nobody who was either a dealer or a collector. So we—the old boys, I suppose one might call us—concluded that someone was buying it as an investment."

"Would it be a good investment at that price?"

Laws thought about it for a while. Then he nodded and said, "As an extremely long-term investment, yes, but there are very few persons around who could afford to do so. Very few."

"The Arabs?"

"A possibility."

"They're buying up everything else," I said.

"I have heard rumors that they are going into rare books as an investment, but they are only rumors."

"How old is the Goodwater daughter?"

"I think she was only a child, or possibly an infant, when Joiner Goodwater made his uranium strike. I suppose she's thirty now, or almost. Why?"

"I was just trying to get a picture of her," I said. "Not married?"

"No."

"Is she odd or eccentric or kooky or somehow unbalanced?"

Laws again shook his head. "No, to the best of my knowledge, at least from what her attorney said, she is a most self-possessed and determined young woman. That was the same impression that I gained by talking to her over the telephone."

"I was wondering why she turned down your offer to provide security measures for the book's transfer?"

"About that she was most clear and most adamant."

"Oh?"

"Yes, she said that the private investigator whom she was sending to pick up the book, a Mr. Jack Marsh—" Laws broke off his sentence as if he were not quite sure how he should complete it.

"What about him?" I said.

"Well, she said that Mr. Marsh was not only a close personal friend, but also highly competent in his field."

"Did you check with the insurance company about him? They must have had some say-so."

"Indeed I did. They said he is not just competent. They said that he is the best there is."

-------------------- **THREE**

Laws and I talked a little longer. I tried to get as many details as I could, and he tried to tell me everything he knew about the theft, which really wasn't very much more than he had already said, and soon we found ourselves going over the same ground.

When I rose to leave he insisted that he give me a personally conducted tour of some of the Library's treasures, and I got to inspect one of the Gutenberg Bibles, plus a second edition of the first book printed in England in 1477, *The Dictes and Sayenges of the Phylosophers,* and the only known presentation copy of Poe's *The Murders in the Rue Morgue,* which I thought was rather neat.

I also made a careful examination of the Library's copy of Pliny's *Historia Naturalis.* It was a thick, heavy folio about eighteen inches tall with perhaps seven hundred pages. Its binding was of heavy boards, probably oak, covered with stamped leather.

I turned to Laws. "The one that was stolen was printed on vellum, you say?"

He nodded. "The only one that was. It increases not only its value enormously, but also its weight. I should say that it weighs approximately forty pounds."

"It would be difficult to fake it, wouldn't it?"

"Fake it?"

"Come up with a forgery," I said.

Laws shook his head. "Virtually impossible but please note that I said virtually. Of late, there have been some really magnificent forgeries, true works of art actually, but mostly they have been forgeries of documents rather than books. To forge a book like this would pose immense technical problems. To reconstitute the vellum and then chemically age it would demand a master craftsman. The binding presents an equally difficult problem, one that is almost insurmountable. But again, I say almost."

"It couldn't be done in, say, a week or ten days."

"No. No it couldn't. Impossible."

I thanked him again for his courtesy, promised that I would keep him informed, shook his hand because he seemed to feel that it would be the polite thing to do, and then left to find a cab to take me back to the hotel.

There weren't any cabs, of course. There weren't any cabs because it was 4:35 in the afternoon and the government workers were streaming out of the Library and the Capitol and the Senate and the House office buildings, and besides that, it was snowing.

They haven't quite yet decided what to do about snow in Washington. When it snows really hard the government shuts down, the schools close, and everybody goes home and waits for it to melt. It was snowing hard now, big fat thick wet flakes that stuck to everything they hit. It looked to me as though it would never end and that Washington might not dig its way out until Mother's Day.

I decided to try for a taxi anyway. The only alternative was a mile-and-a-half walk back to the hotel. My reasoning was that if I were going to catch pneumonia, I needed to conserve my strength. So I stood there at the corner of First and Independence Southeast and yelled and waved my arms and whistled and attracted a number of amused looks and smug smiles from homeward-bound commuters, but no taxi.

I was just about to give up when the black Plymouth sedan let go with a growl from its siren, frightened some cars out of its way, and edged over to the curb. Its right-hand door opened, and I heard a voice say, "Get in, St. Ives. You look ridiculous."

I brushed some of the snow off, got in quickly, and said, "You promised not to be late again."

"Still the wise-ass," the man behind the wheel said and threatened a couple of more cars with a growl from the siren. The cars fell back, and he squeezed the Plymouth sedan over into the slow-moving traffic.

His name was Herbert Fastnaught, and in the six or seven years since I had last seen him he had lost his youth. Some policemen do that, grow old in a week, and it seemed to have happened to Fastnaught. When I had last seen him he had been a boyish, pink-cheeked, gum-chewing detective sergeant in the Metropolitan Police Department's robbery squad. Now he chewed on a thick unlit cigar, and the pink cheeks had sagged down into heavy jowls, and the curly blond hair that I remembered was turning grey at the sides and thin on top. He looked forty-five, although I knew that he couldn't be much more than thirty-seven.

"I thought you'd be at the Madison," Fastnaught said, not looking at me, but staring at the bumper of the car ahead. "So I called there, but they said you weren't registered and I thought to myself, the Hay Adams, that's about the next most expensive hotel in town, and sure enough, you were registered there, but you weren't in. So I called Laws, and he said you'd just left. I took a chance that you couldn't find a cab and there you were waving your arms around and looking silly."

"I hear you made lieutenant," I said. "Congratulations."

"Thanks. You ain't changed much."

"I exercise, try to watch my diet, and drink a lot of Scotch," I said. "It does wonders."

"This book you're go-betweening."

"The Pliny."

"Yeah, the Pliny book. You can buy me some expense account Scotch, and we'll have a little talk about it."

"All right. You still in robbery?"

"Nah, I'm not in robbery anymore."

"What happened to that partner of yours, Demeter?"

"Demeter? Well, Demeter was all set to retire, he had three weeks to go, and then he goes into this place that he's got no business going into, a pad over on Ninth and T, and some dude takes the left side of his head off with a shotgun, just like that, and him three weeks away from retirement."

"I'm sorry to hear it," I said.

"Yeah. So was his wife." Fastnaught took out a disposable lighter and used it to light his cigar. He blew some smoke at the windshield, still not looking at me, still looking at the car ahead. "What about you, you still in New York?"

"Still there."

"You aren't married again, are you?"

"No." I said.

"I didn't think so. I got married."

"Really? Congratulations."

"Don't bother," he said. "It's not working out too good."

We didn't seem to have any more old times to catch up on, so we drove in silence until we got to the hotel. The bar we chose was downstairs, a small place that was presided over by an elderly bartender and a waiter who might have been his uncle. There were only two other persons in the bar, a young man and a girl, but they were unaware of anything except each other.

Both Fastnaught and I ordered Scotch and water, and after the old man served the drinks Fastnaught took a big, thirsty swallow of his, and then took another one, quickly, as if the first swallow hadn't done for him quite what he had hoped it would do.

"I'm drinking too much," he said.

"So is everybody."

"Nah, I'm getting close to the edge. I can tell. I've watched too many guys get close to the edge and then slide over. I don't know whether I'm going to slide over or not. Either you do or you don't. I worry about it."

"Drink something you don't like," I said. "If you like Scotch, switch to rye or Irish."

"Does it help?"

"I don't know," I said. "The guys who told me about it are all in A.A. now."

"Maybe I'll do that. Just quit altogether."

"Maybe you will."

"But not right now," he said and signaled the old waiter for another round.

After it came, Fastnaught took a swallow, relit his cigar, which had gone out, and blew some smoke up into the air. I noticed that he inhaled the cigar smoke. "Like I said," he told me, "I'm not in robbery anymore. In fact, I haven't been in robbery for five years. I was in homicide for quite a while, which was kinda interesting, but now I'm in the government liaison section. In fact, I am the government liaison section, me and a girl who answers the phone and does the typing."

"I don't think I'm going to congratulate you again," I said.

"No. Don't. You wanta know what the government liaison section does? Well, it tries to make sure that if somebody gets busted who shouldn't, the public doesn't have to get all worried about it. Hell of a job for a grown man, isn't it?"

"Does it keep you busy?" I said because I felt I should say something.

"There are about three or four thousand people in this town who, if you're an ordinary cop, it's better not to mess with. You got the members of Congress, that's one. Then there's the Cabinet, the other government big shots, and the diplomatic corps. And then there's the heavy money crowd, which is about the same as it is in any town. Well, sometimes these people get in jams. Maybe they get tanked up and drive their car into the reflecting pool, or maybe they knock their wife or girl friend around a little, or maybe they go pick up a nigger whore over on Thirteenth or Fourteenth and get in trouble with her pimp. My job is to sort of smooth these things over and maybe, if it's not too bad, keep it out of the papers and off of the TV." Fastnaught took another big swallow of his drink and a gloomy look settled over his face. "I've had what maybe you could call some notable failures."

"I can think of a couple," I said.

"But most of the time you know what I do?"

"What?"

"I fix parking tickets."

"Well, I guess somebody has to do it."

Fastnaught shook his head. "I gotta get out of it. I either gotta get out of it, or I gotta quit. And that's where you come in, St. Ives."

I shook my head. "You know how I work," I said.

"Yeah, I know. You stay in the go-between business because you've built yourself up a reputation with the thieves. They know you'll do what you say you're gonna do. And the cops don't mind working with you because after you get through go-betweening, you tell 'em anything they wanta know, and the thieves don't mind that because by then they've got the money, and they're spending it down in Mexico or someplace. Isn't that right?"

"That's close."

"Well, when the book got stolen the department touched base with me because the Library of Congress is just what its name says it is, it's part of Congress and if possible Congress don't want something like this

40

written up in the papers, because it might give somebody else ideas about how they could do the same thing."

"It wasn't stolen from the Library," I said. "It was stolen after it left the Library."

"Yeah, I know all that. But I sort of brushed over that when I made my pitch down at headquarters."

"What pitch?"

"I told them that I'd worked with you before and I knew how you operated. I told them I thought I'd better be assigned to this thing full-time and stick close to you, and when you got through paying the quarter of a million and got the book back all nice and safe, then I could make my move and box in whoever stole the book before he got the chance to spend the money. Well, they didn't buy it."

"Too bad."

"Yeah. Well, maybe you've sorta guessed that I don't sit too well over there on Indiana Avenue. My name isn't mud over there, it's shit, and maybe it's my fault and maybe it isn't, but I know if I don't work a big one like this, something they'll have to sit up and notice, then I'm gonna be fixing parking tickets for the rest of my life. Either that or I quit and I don't wanta quit because I don't know what else I could do."

"Did you ever think of going into selling?" I said. "You'd make a terrific salesman."

"Funny. Jesus, you're real funny, St. Ives, you break me up."

"You worked it somehow," I said. "I know you worked it, or otherwise you wouldn't be sitting here telling me about it."

"Yeah, I worked it. About a year ago I got a Senator out of a jam. A real bad jam, the kind that if I hadn've got him out of Jack Anderson would have told all about it in about eight or nine hundred papers. Well, nobody knows about this jam except me and the Senator and a couple of other parties who aren't gonna give him any trouble anymore. I never reported it in like I'm supposed to and the Senator's sort of grateful, if you know what I mean."

"The Senator put the squeeze on for you."

"That's right. He put it on in a real smooth way so that they didn't even know he was putting it on for me. This morning they called me back in and said that they'd changed their minds, and that maybe I'd better liaise with you after all. Liaise isn't really a word, is it?"

"I don't think so."

"They use it all the time down there, but I didn't think it was really a word."

I leaned back in my chair and looked at him. The drinks had spread to his face, giving it a shiny, wet flush. He was huddled over his glass, clutching it with both hands. The cigar had gone dead in his fingers. There was a wet stain on his tie. He looked tired and middle-aged and a little desperate.

"What do you want?" I said.

"I want the thief."

I shook my head. "Not from me. I don't serve them up. You know that."

"Your rules," he said. "We play by your rules."

"My rules sometimes give the thief an edge."

"Let me worry about that."

"All right," I said. "I will."

-------------------- **FOUR**

The thief called at 8:32 that night, and I couldn't decide whether the voice belonged to a countertenor or a low contralto. Whoever it was seemed to have put something into his or her mouth to alter the voice. All you really have to do, if you want to do that, is stick your finger into your mouth and talk around it. But some of them use marbles and handkerchiefs and even voice-altering devices, although none of them works much better than a finger.

"Are you ready to start?" the voice said.

"You're a little early," I said. "The insurance man hasn't got in from California yet. I don't know if he's bringing the money with him, or if he's arranged to get it from a bank here."

"His plane touched down at Dulles three minutes ago," the voice said.

"I wasn't even sure he could land in all this snow."

"The plane had to circle for an hour."

"You do keep in touch."

"That's right, we do," the voice said. "We'd also like to take a look at you."

"I'm not so much," I said. "Five-eleven, a hundred and sixty-five pounds, fair complexion, dark blond hair, and shy brown eyes."

"That's nice," the voice said. "At nine o'clock you can take your brown eyes down to the lobby where a dinner meeting will have just let out. At exactly nine-oh-five we want you to go over to the newsstand and buy a copy of *Time* magazine, a Hershey bar, and two packs of Kents. Then we want you to go right back up to your room."

"Then what?"

"We'll be in touch," the voice said. After that there was a click, and the phone went dead.

Because I had some time to kill and because life has taught me not to be quite as trusting as I was when I was six, I called Dulles and found out that a United flight from Los Angeles had indeed touched down just a few minutes before, after having circled the airport for nearly an hour. After that I stood at the window and watched it snow on the statues in Lafayette Square.

At 9:01 I was down in the lobby. A small crowd of fifty or so well-dressed people were milling about, putting on their coats, and telling each other what a wonderful speech it had been and how glad they were that they had braved the snow to hear it. I stood there in the lobby trying to decide if there were a politician whom I would go out to hear on a snowy night, or even a nice warm one, decided that there wasn't, and then moved slowly through the crowd over to the newsstand. I stood there for another moment and looked around casually, trying to sense rather than see whether there was anyone watching me. But there were too many people still putting on their coats and chattering to each other about the speech and the snow. I could neither sense nor see anyone staring at me, so I looked at my watch and saw that it was 9:05.

I took a copy of *Time* from the magazine rack, told the newsstand clerk I would like a Hershey bar and two packs of Kents, paid for them, and moved back through the thinning crowd to the elevator. I looked around again but nobody was even looking my way. They were all still talking to each other, and none of them seemed to care whether I went up to my room and took a nap or out into Sixteenth Street and built a snowman.

Back up in my room I turned on the TV set and ate the Hershey bar while I watched a rerun of a cops and robbers program that seemed to be taking place out in Los Angeles under smog-alert conditions. I turned the TV set off after a few minutes and settled down with *Time*, reading it from back to front as I always did. I was about halfway through the magazine and learning all about what names had made news last week when the phone rang.

A deep male voice asked me if I were Mr. St. Ives, and when I said I was he said that he was Max Spivey, that he was a vice-president with the Pacifica insurance company, that he had just had a rotten flight in from Los Angeles, and a even worse trip in from Dulles, and that he needed to see me, but that he needed a drink even worse.

"Do you drink Scotch?"

"I drink anything."

"I've got some J and B up here that you're welcome to."

"I'll be up in five minutes," he said.

He was knocking on the door in a little less than that. His deep voice went with his size, which was large, very large, even massive. He held out his hand and said, "I'm Max Spivey," and his voice seemed to rumble up out of his chest.

"Philip St. Ives," I said as my hand vanished inside of his.

"I've heard about you," he said. "You're supposed to be good."

"Thanks," I said. "Sit down anywhere."

The room seemed to shrink in size by half after he came in. He looked around and nodded at the bed. "I'll use that," he said. "I don't like to sit on hotel chairs until I've tested them."

He wasn't much less than seven feet tall, possibly four inches less, maybe even five, but no more than that. He sat down carefully on the bed, but the springs protested anyhow, and it seemed to embarrass him a little. Even though he was huge he was well proportioned, all 275 pounds of him at least, and when he leaned forward to rest his arms on his knees his pants legs stretched tight revealing thighs as thick as telephone poles. They went with the rest of him.

"It's a nice hotel," he said when I came back out of the bathroom carrying two glasses. "I decided to get a room here when your lawyer said that this is where you'd be staying."

"They keep it up," I said. "How do you want your Scotch? I've got water, but no ice."

"Just pour some in a glass," he said.

"How's that?" I said and handed him a water tumbler that was a third full.

He said that was fine, waited until he was sure that I had a drink of my own, raised his glass in a small salute, and then knocked back half of his drink in a gulp.

He was somewhere past thirty-five, a year or two past it, which was long enough to have got him accustomed to the idea that he was going to have to make his way in a world that was designed for a smaller race. His moves were smooth and careful, almost delicate, as if he were afraid that he might squash something if he moved too fast.

If he hadn't been so big, his looks wouldn't have turned any heads. Although he wasn't exactly ugly there was a bit too much chin and forehead, and something should have been done for his nose which arced down and to the left toward a thick-lipped mouth that turned up at one end and down at the other as if it couldn't decide whether to snarl or smile. But when he did smile, as he did now after having drunk some of my Scotch, it was a merry one that showed a lot of splendid white teeth.

If you looked at him only casually, you might take him for just another huge hulk of a man who hadn't quite grown up to be a giant. But if you looked again, you would have noticed his eyes, and then you would have known that somewhere inside that huge frame was a cool, watchful intelligence that liked to puzzle things out on its own. They were green eyes, almost sea green, and what they had seen so far of life may have robbed them of most of their warmth.

After he had taken another swallow of his drink, Spivey produced a pack of unfiltered Camels, lit one, and then used his thumb to indicate the window.

"We're not exactly used to snow out in L.A.," he said.

"Well, they're not too sure what it is here either."

"Yeah, I took a cab in from the airport. It cost me twenty bucks and I think that half the time we were going sideways. A hell of a trip." He took another swallow of his drink. "You heard from them yet?"

"The thief—or thieves?"

"Yeah. I figure it's two. At least two. It would take two to get through Jack Marsh."

"I understand that you're pretty high on him."

He nodded. "He's one of the best private operators on the coast. I guess we've used him maybe a dozen times."

"In what capacity?"

"You know much about us?"

I shook my head. "Not much. Just what my lawyer told me. You seem to be taking away some funny business from Lloyds of London."

"You mean the tits and ass stuff?"

"Is that what you call it?"

"Uh-huh. The guy who started us doing it about twenty-five years ago used to be a talent agent, one of the top agents in L.A. And he kept on being an agent until somebody took the trouble to explain to him one day just how a life insurance company works—I mean really works. Well, as you probably know, a life com-

48

pany's a license to steal, and I'm not giving away any trade secrets."

"No," I said, "you're not."

"Well, this guy who used to be an agent—his name's Ronnie Saperstein and now he's chairman of the board —well, the first thing he did was to go looking for a small life company, and he ran across Pacifica Life and Casualty up in Santa Barbara, which was just sort of noodling along and dozing in the sunshine up there. Well, he worked a deal with them and the first thing he did was to insure each of his clients—he had about thirty of them then—for one million dollars each on a special group rate. Now that was one hell of a chunk of business for a little company like Pacifica was then, and the next thing you know Ronnie's a vice-president. Well, he used to have this one female client who was still a pretty fair actress but whose career had sort of hit the skids. But she still had this terrific set of jugs. So Ronnie insures them for five million bucks—each. Well, she made the wire services on that and the next thing you know every flack in town is wanting to insure everything from their clients' crossed eyes to their barks. And that's how the tits and ass business got started."

"But you're primarily a life company?"

"Primarily. The casualty's sort of a sideline, but it makes us a lot of money because over the years the tits and ass publicity, believe it or not, has drawn us just one hell of a lot of good conservative business—museums, storage companies, people like that."

"What have you used Jack Marsh on, casualty or life?"

"Both," Spivey said. "But mostly life. Whenever

some guy gets the notion to insure his wife for a couple of hundred thousand and the wife gets killed in a car wreck the next week, well, we sort of like Jack to go talk to the guy. He's pretty good at it."

"I understand he's a good friend of the Goodwater woman who owns the Pliny book."

"I guess Maude Goodwater and he are a little more than just good friends," Spivey said. "They're living together."

"I also understand that it was okay with you that she sent Marsh to pick up the book."

"If we could've chosen between him and a company of marines, I think we probably would've still taken him. He's that good. Or at least I think so."

"He picked up the book yesterday," I said.

"Yesterday morning."

"And the next thing you know, somebody with a high voice and a mouthful of marbles is on the phone to your company claiming that they've got the book and that they'll sell it back to you for a quarter of a million. What'd they say about our Jack Marsh?"

"Who do you figure it is," he said. "A woman or a guy trying to sound like a woman?"

"I don't know," I said.

"Well, whoever it was said that Jack was safe."

"Is that all?"

"And that they'd let him go when they got the money."

"Did you believe her?"

"Her?"

"That's what I call the voice," I said. "Her."

Spivey looked down at his glass. It was empty. I took

50

the bottle and poured him some more whiskey. He tasted it and this time he rolled it around in his mouth before swallowing it. "It's a kidnapping, too, isn't it?"

"Uh-huh. It looks that way."

"I've never dealt with kidnappers before," he said. "I've had some dealings with the common garden variety of hardcases, but no kidnappers. You've done business with them before, I guess."

"A few times."

"How was it?"

"Nasty."

"I imagine."

"They kill them about half the time," I said. "Maybe a little more than half."

"You figure that's what Marsh's chances are, fifty-fifty?"

"I don't know," I said. "They're not ransoming him. They're asking a quarter of a million for the book, not for him."

"That's a lot of money," Spivey said.

"It's even more when you add on my twenty-five thousand."

"I'm not forgetting that."

"My lawyer gets ten percent of it."

"Is that how you work it?" Spivey said. He seemed interested.

I nodded. "I was just wondering. You know him. Would a quarter of a million dollars be a whole lot of money to Jack Marsh?"

Spivey stared at me. "That's crossed my mind," he said.

"Well?"

"I'm not sure. People do funny things for that much money. Jack's people. Maybe he decided to do something funny."

"It's a possibility, huh?"

"Yeah," Spivey said. "That's just what it is. A possibility."

"What about the money?"

"We made arrangements with the Riggs bank here," he said. "I can get it any time tomorrow any way the thieves want it. They didn't say how or when that would be, did they?"

"No."

"What about the cops?"

"They're trying to keep a lid on it," I said. "The guy who's in charge of the lid is a Lieutenant Fastnaught."

"You know him?"

"I worked with him one time before."

"How is he?"

"He's all right."

"That's not exactly the warmest recommendation I ever heard."

"Well, let's put it this way," I said. "He's better than some and worse than others."

"One of those, huh?"

I nodded. "One of those."

"That leaves one other thing," he said.

"What?"

"The FBI. If it's a kidnapping, it's in their ball park, isn't it?"

"That's how I understand it."

"Has this Washington cop, what's his name—"

"Fastnaught."

"Yeah, Fastnaught. Has he filled them in?"

"I didn't ask," I said. "I didn't ask because I didn't want to remind him if he hadn't."

"Sounds as though you don't much care for the FBI."

I shrugged. "They sometimes come on pretty strong."

"So you wouldn't care if they weren't brought in?"

"No, I wouldn't care."

"Well, if you don't care, then I don't care, and I don't suppose whoever stole it would care either."

"No," I said. "They wouldn't care at all."

"That leaves Jack Marsh. What do you think?"

"Maybe he's already past caring."

Spivey stood up. "Yeah," he said, "maybe he is."

──────────────────── FIVE

I was up and about the Lord's business the next morning by 7:30 and so was the thief, who called at 7:35.

"You awake?" the high voice said.

"I'm awake."

"You talk to Spivey?"

"Yes. Last night."

"What about the money?"

"He can get it when the bank opens. They open here at nine. How do you want it?"

The voice didn't have to think about that. "Old hundreds and twenties. Make sure they're old."

"No fifties?"

"All right, some fifties. But not too many."

"How about a hundred thousand in twenties, another hundred thousand in one-hundreds, and the rest in fifties. That'll make a neat little package."

"How neat?"

"It'll fit into either a large attaché case or a small suitcase. I'll throw in whichever one you want as part of the service."

"Make it a small suitcase."

"All right. What next?"

"Next after you get the money is that you be back in your hotel room by ten. If we don't call then, we'll call you at eleven."

"What about Jack Marsh?" I said.

"What about him?"

"It would be nice if I could talk to him. You know, see whether he's had his breakfast yet."

"Do you know him?"

"No."

"Then you wouldn't know if you're talking to him or just to some guy who said he was Jack Marsh, would you?"

"No, I don't suppose I would."

"So there's not much point in your talking to him."

"I think Max Spivey would like to talk to him. He knows Marsh."

"We don't talk to anyone but you, St. Ives. Get that straight."

"All right, but you can at least tell me how Marsh is."

"Sure, I'll tell you how he is. He's fine. Does that satisfy you?"

"It might satisfy me, but not the cops."

"No cops. That's why we sent for you, because they said you wouldn't run any cops in."

"I don't run them in, but that doesn't mean I can always keep them out. Especially the FBI."

"I'll tell you what you can tell the FBI."

"What?"

"You can tell them that if they want Marsh back all safe and sound, they'd better stay out of it until we get our money. Is that clear?"

"It's clear."

"We'll be in touch," the high voice said, and once again the phone went dead.

I hung up and crossed over to the window. It was no longer snowing but it was still overcast. There seemed to be about six or seven inches of snow covering Lafayette Square. There was nobody in the square except for a woman, all bundled up in a brown scarf and brown coat, who was feeding bread to some pigeons out of a paper bag. The pigeons reminded me that I was hungry and that I hadn't had any coffee, so I went back to the phone and called Max Spivey to tell him what the thief had told me and to see whether he would like to join me in some breakfast.

While I waited for Spivey in the dining room I drank coffee and scanned the *Washington Post,* which said that there was a fifty-fifty chance of its snowing some more and that the schools in Washington and the surrounding counties would be closed, although the federal government offices would remain open. They ran a picture on the front page of a massive traffic tieup out on Shirley Highway, and the caption said that some drivers had been stuck in it until nearly nine o'clock the night before.

Spivey came in and sat down, and the waiter hurried over and poured him some coffee and took our orders. Spivey said that he wanted orange juice, four eggs over easy, ham, hash brown potatoes, if they had them, and a large order of toast. I said that I would like some rye toast and a soft-boiled egg.

"You on a diet?" Spivey said after the waiter went away.

"No, it's just that breakfast isn't my favorite meal. It doesn't offer enough variety, I guess."

"Big as I am I have to stoke the furnace. But you've got a point there. About variety, I mean."

"I was trying to think whether I'd ever run across your name before," I said.

"Like where?"

"Maybe on the sports page."

"You mean because of my size?"

"Well, you're big enough and you move okay."

He shook his head. "I got a trick left knee. I played some football in high school but my knee went in my senior year and that did it. I boxed a little in college but I never took it anywhere."

"How long have you been with Pacifica?"

He thought about it. "About twelve years now. I started out in sales, in the tits and ass stuff, as a matter of fact, and then I switched to claims and I guess I was pretty good at it because they made me a vice-president a couple of years ago." He looked at me. "You might say I'm the vice-president in charge of trouble."

"You get a lot of it?"

"Enough. When the economy goes sour, the phony claims start to rise. People lose their jobs and go through their savings, if they've got any. Then they borrow every cent they can, and when that's gone they sit around and look at each other and wonder what the hell they're going to do next. They have fantasies, you know. They sit there with no money and wonder what it would be like if the other one stepped in front of a truck and all that insurance money suddenly fell into their lap and how noble and brave they'd be at the funeral. Well, you know what happens. They rig up something, but they usually rig it up too fancy, and the homicide boys move right in. But sometimes they keep it simple, and it looks like just what they wanted it to look like, an accident, and the cops say it's accidental death and so does the coroner after the autopsy. Everybody knows it's an accident except us."

"How do you know it isn't?"

He shook his head. "We just know. It doesn't smell right. It doesn't feel right. It doesn't even taste right—you know what I mean? So we run it through the computer again just to get the odds on that particular accident happening to that particular person at that particular time. Then we sit there and look at what the computer says, and then we look at each other. And sometimes, when the smell is bad and the taste is sour and the computer results are a little colicky, we call in somebody like Jack Marsh and tell him to pick up where the cops left off and see what he can find."

"And he's pretty good at it?" I said.

"He's got a feel for it. Some do and some don't."

"What's his background?"

"I knew him in college at USC. Then he went into the Army and they put him into counter-intelligence. In Germany. He must have been good at it because he came out a captain. After that he tried college again, but it didn't work out, so he quit and went with the

L.A. police. It was about then, about ten years ago, that he looked me up and every once in a while we'd have a few drinks together. I was still in sales then. In fact, I'd just sold a big policy to Joiner Goodwater on his rare book collection. It was quite a collection back then."

"So I've heard."

"Well, I'd met Maude Goodwater, and just to be polite because it was a big policy I'd asked her and her father out to lunch. For some reason the old man had to cancel out, and it was just Maude and me. Well, we went to this place, and there was Jack Marsh at the bar on his day off so I asked him to join us. That's how they met. I introduced them."

"And they've been together ever since?"

Spivey shook his head. "No, they went together for a couple of years, and then Maude met somebody else and married him. It lasted about five years, I guess. He wasn't much. I think he was in public relations for a bank or something. Anyway, she left him, and then when her father died it was in all the papers, and Jack Marsh saw it and called her up. They started seeing each other again, and about a year ago they started living together."

"But Marsh wasn't with the Los Angeles police anymore?"

Spivey shook his head. "It was too slow for him. I don't mean the action, I mean the promotion and the pay and all. Jack picked up some pretty expensive tastes when he was in Europe. So he quit the cops and went with a big insurance company as a claims investigator and really found his niche, I guess. He was good and he was mean, and the company liked that. He was so good, in fact, that he got an offer for a hell of a lot more money from another company. But instead of taking it, he resigned, and set up his own shop as a private investigator specializing in claims work. He did real fine right from the start. He makes a lot of money. He should. He charges enough."

Spivey wiped up the last of his eggs with a piece of toast and popped it into his mouth. "I've been talking a lot," he said. "I must be nervous."

I thought he looked about as nervous as the floor. "You want some more coffee?"

He shook his head. "We might as well go get it."

The waiter brought over the check, and Spivey reached for it and signed his name and room number to it. He left a dollar bill for the waiter, and we got our topcoats and caught a cab outside of the hotel.

The cab driver was a Nigerian, and he had the heater up as high as it would go. He complained about the snow and the cold and told us about how nice and warm it was in Lagos and how on days like this he wished he were back there instead of here where he was studying to be an engineer.

He was a terrible snow driver, possibly because it was the second time he had ever seen any, and we went into a couple of breathtaking skids before we pulled up in front of a People's drugstore. Spivey waited in the cab while I went in and bought a small, cheap plastic suitcase for $4.98 plus tax. After two more skids, one little one and one big one which made me close my eyes, the driver let us off at the Riggs bank on Pennsylvania Avenue across from the Treasury building.

In the bank Spivey asked for a Mr. Bilanow who was a vice-president and who, like all bankers, wasn't at all pleased with the notion of parting with $250,000 that he couldn't charge any interest on. He also wanted to make sure that Spivey was indeed Max Spivey of the Pacifica Life and Casualty Company, and it was only after Spivey produced his driver's license, three credit cards, and a letter of introduction from the Bank of America, which was the corresponding bank in Los Angeles, that Bilanow said, "Well, yes, Mr. Spivey, everything seems to be in order. Now how would you like it?"

Spivey looked at me. "Old bills," I said. "A hundred thousand in twenties, a hundred thousand in hundreds, and the rest in fifties."

Bilanow wrote it down in a neat hand, excused himself and left us sitting at his desk while he went over to a teller's cage. He was gone about ten minutes, and when he returned he was carrying a wire basket that was full of money. He put the basket down on the desk. "I suggest you count it, Mr. Spivey," he said and then stepped back as though he wanted to be out of the way.

Spivey looked at me. "That's just one hell of a lot of money, isn't it?"

"For one book it is," I said.

"Or for anything else. Let's count it."

I put the suitcase up on the desk, and we started counting the money into it. It was all in one- and five-thousand-dollar packets, and it nearly filled the suitcase.

"Is it old enough?" Spivey said.

"It looks all right," I said.

"You're the judge," he said and closed the suitcase.

Bilanow stepped forward with some papers for Spivey to sign. While he was signing them, Bilanow said, "Mr. Spivey, I offer the suggestion that one of our security people accompany you back to your hotel. It's only a suggestion, of course."

"Thanks, but I don't think that's necessary."

"You could ask somebody to go out and get us a cab though," I said. "I'd rather not stand around on a corner trying to hail one with a quarter of a million dollars under my arm."

Bilanow said that he would see to it and left to find somebody who liked to go out and hail cabs in near-freezing weather. I hefted the suitcase and then put it back down on the desk.

"How much does it weigh?" Spivey said.

"Exactly?"

"Well, close."

"Fourteen pounds and maybe twelve or thirteen ounces. That's not counting the suitcase."

"Jesus, how can you be so sure?"

"There're four hundred ninety bills to the pound. There're seven thousand bills in there and after that you just do a little long division in your head."

"Yeah, I guess you would know about things like that."

"Uh-huh. I would."

"You want to take it over now?"

"Not yet."

"Well, when are you going to take it over?"

I pushed the suitcase a little toward Spivey. "When the thief tells me where to bring it," I said. "That's when I'll take it over."

62

―――――――――――――――― SIX

Spivey and I were back in the hotel by a quarter to ten. I watched while he arranged for the suitcase to be put into the hotel's safe, and then we went back up to my room. Once again he chose the bed to sit on.

"We just wait now, huh?" he said.

"That's right. We wait. Would you like some coffee?"

"Yeah, I think I would."

I called room service and asked them to send up a large pot of coffee and two cups. Spivey leaned back on the bed, supporting himself on his elbows. "I've been thinking," he said.

"About what?"

"About Marsh. I've been thinking we ought to lean on them a little. Unless they agree to deliver Marsh along with the book, the deal's off."

"What if they can't?"

"You mean what if Marsh is already dead?"

"Yes."

"We'd better make sure that he isn't."

"I already asked them to let you talk to them. They said no."

"Ask them again."

"And if they say no again?"

Spivey raised himself up and leaned forward toward me. "Then I think we'd better turn it over to the cops or the FBI. I've got a couple of reasons for that. One of them is that Jack's a friend of mine. The second one's a little more crass. It wouldn't read too well if the word got out that an insurance company got a guy killed just to get an old book back. That wouldn't read too well at all."

"If he's already dead," I said, "there's nothing you can do about it."

"No, but maybe the cops can. Or like I said, the FBI."

"And if he's not dead?"

"Then we play along with the thieves."

"All right," I said. "I'll tell them that unless they let you talk to Marsh the deal's off."

"Yeah. I think that's the way it'll have to go."

After that we didn't have much to say to each other. I looked at my watch. It was five until ten. I forced myself not to look at it again until the phone rang, and when it did it was exactly ten o'clock.

I picked up the phone and said hello and the high voice said, "You got the money?"

"I've got the money, but I've also got a problem."

There was a silence and then the voice said, "What kind of a problem?"

"The problem is Jack Marsh. Unless Max Spivey talks to him and makes sure that he's okay, the deal's off. We'll just turn it over to the cops or the FBI—or maybe both."

There was another silence. "You say Spivey's there?"

"He's here."

"Okay. We're going to let him talk to Marsh. But nothing cute, you understand?"

"I understand," I said and waved Spivey over to the phone. He took it and held it away from his ear so that I could listen.

"Jack?" he said.

A man's voice said, "Who's this, Max?"

"Yeah, how's it going, fellah?"

"It's gone better," the voice said. I looked at Spivey. He nodded sharply at me to indicate that it was Marsh's voice.

"Are they treating you all right?"

"Yeah, they're treating me all right. It's not exactly the—"

Marsh's voice ended, there was a pause, and then the high voice came back on, thick and muffled and hard to understand. "Put St. Ives back on," the voice said.

Spivey handed me the phone. I said, "Hold it a second," put my hand over the mouthpiece and said to Spivey, "That was Marsh, right?"

"Right," Spivey said.

"Okay," I said into the phone. "What's next?"

"Next, you gotta understand that we're not exactly stupid," the voice said. "Your friend Marsh doesn't know what we look like or what we talk like because if he did know that, he'd already be dead. Maybe you've noticed I've got sort of a funny voice."

"I've noticed," I said.

"Yeah, well, it's not mine. And that's why Marsh is gonna come out of this okay, because he doesn't know what we look like or talk like or even where he is. So let's stop worrying about him and start worrying about doing some business."

"Okay," I said. "I'm ready to start worrying when you are."

"You know where Haines Point is?"

"I'm not sure," I said. "I think so."

"It's at the end of that long, skinny park that goes out into the Potomac just sort of south and east of the tidal basin. On one side's the Potomac. On the other side's the Washington Channel."

"Okay. I've got it."

"At midnight we want you to drive to the very tip of Haines Point in a Ford sedan. You can rent one."

"All right."

"Over to the right will be either a green or a blue Chevy Impala, and don't worry about memorizing its license because we haven't stolen it yet."

"I won't bother then."

"Good. Now we want you to go past the Chevy about fifty feet and park. All you have to do is just sit there, except that you gotta get out once and go around and unlock your trunk because that's where the money's gonna be. Then you get back in your car. You got it?"

"You're doing fine."

"Somebody will get out of the Chevy, go over to your car, put the book in the trunk, and take the money out. Then they'll go back to the Chevy. You can get out and check that the book's there. Then we just want you to get back in your car again and sort of wander away. How do you like it?"

"I can see that you've put a lot of thought into it," I said. "But there're a couple of little things that bother me."

"Such as?"

"Such as I'm buying, not selling. That means I'd like to inspect the merchandise before I part with the money. So why don't we just reverse the procedure? You leave your trunk open with the book in it. I'll park fifty feet behind you and make sure it's the book I want and not just some old copy of *Wind in the Willows*. If it's what I want, I'll put the money in your trunk and then go back to my car. I'll be fifty feet away and it'll be dark. I won't be able to see who gets out of your car and goes around to make sure that I've left the money. After that, I'll take your suggestion. I'll just sort of wander away."

There was a silence on the telephone, and finally the high voice said, "All right, we'll do it your way. There's not much difference anyhow."

"I've got one more little problem," I said.

"What?"

"Jack Marsh. I'd like to get him back along with the book."

"Yeah, well, I'm afraid Jack's gonna have to be our ace. If everything goes just like we talked about, well, we'll turn Jack loose someplace and make sure he's got cab fare, and he'll show up about one or maybe two tomorrow morning. But we've gotta keep Jack around just to make sure that you don't try anything cute, or the cops don't, or even the FBI like you were

67

talking about. If everything cracks out like it's supposed to, then Jack's gonna be okay. If it doesn't and you try something funny, well, maybe you get one of us, but Jack's gonna be in real bad trouble. You got it?"

"I've got it," I said.

"Swell," the voice said. "Midnight tonight." After that, the phone went dead, and I hung up.

Before I could tell Spivey what had been said there was a knock on the door. I went over and opened it. It was the room service waiter with the coffee. He came in with a cheery good morning, put the tray on the desk, and presented me with the bill. I signed it, added a tip, and the waiter left.

"How do you like your coffee?"

"Black."

I poured two cups and handed Spivey one of them. "They're going to keep Marsh as insurance," I said. "When they get the money, they'll turn him loose. They say."

"What do you think?"

I put a spoonful of sugar into my coffee and stirred it. "I don't know. They said that he doesn't know what they look like. That means that they're two of them, I suppose. Maybe three. We don't know much about any of it really. For instance, we don't know how they got Marsh. Maybe they jumped him from behind and banged him over the head before he got a look at them. After that maybe they blindfolded him, or put a sack over his head, and stuck him away in a room someplace, and the only time they talked in front of him was when they changed their voices."

Spivey didn't say anything for a moment. He

68

seemed to be thinking. "They wouldn't have to talk to him, would they? I mean all they'd have to say is, 'Here,' when they gave him some food. Or, 'There,' when they let him go to the john." The thought seemed to cheer Spivey up. "What I mean is that maybe it's just as they say. Maybe they can afford to let him go because he knows fuck all about what they look like or sound like or who they are."

"Or maybe that's just what they want us to think," I said.

Spivey stared at me and then nodded. "You mean just to make us go ahead with the deal?"

"That's right. Kidnappers are weird. They're not like other thieves. Kidnappers steal people, which means that they're usually more emotionally and mentally screwed up than your ordinary thief. When your ordinary thief steals something—especially money—then that's the end of it. If it's not money, then he has to fence it, but he does that through somebody who's just as crooked as he is. Or sometimes he'll sell it back to the owner, working through somebody like me. The owner's very attached to whatever's been stolen, or the insurance company wants to cut its losses, so they're willing to pay to get it back and no questions asked. But a kidnap victim, unless it's an infant, can remember what he saw, and he can tell all about what he remembers. So, as often as not, the kidnap victim winds up dead."

"So you still think Marsh has about a fifty-fifty chance?" Spivey said.

"About that. Unless we're dealing with a new variety of kidnapper."

"Well, are we?" he said. "I mean how do they seem to stack up with the ones you've dealt with before?"

I thought about it for a moment. "About average," I said. "The switch they've suggested is simple. Sometimes they dream up extremely complicated ones that call for a dozen moves. The less experienced the thief, the more complicated the switch. So I think whoever we're dealing with has had some experience and maybe that's in Marsh's favor. It probably is."

Spivey finished his coffee. He held out his cup, and I poured him some more. "It could be really simple, couldn't it?" he said. "I mean maybe it'll be so simple that all you'll have to do to earn your twenty-five thousand is take a little drive at midnight. Then you can come back here, and we can sit up and have a few drinks and wait for Marsh to drop by and join us. If that's the way it'll go, I can see why you're in the business."

"That's how I have to think it will go," I said. "Otherwise I wouldn't do it."

"But it doesn't always go like that?"

"No."

"Things happen, huh?"

"Sometimes," I said. "Not often, but sometimes. They happen often enough to make what I do not an overly crowded field."

"You carry a gun?"

"No."

"I think if I were doing what you do, I'd carry one."

"If you carry a gun, it should mean that you're willing to shoot somebody."

"And you're not?"

"Not over money," I said.

-------------------- **SEVEN**

After finishing his second cup of coffee Spivey said he had to go back to his room to call his office and bring them up to date. After he left I finished reading the copy of *Time* that I had bought the night before. I even read the column that listed the editors and the writers and the researchers to see whether anyone I knew was still working for it. Nobody was, and I wondered why they had quit or if they had been fired and where they were working now.

That brought me up to noon and I called Spivey to see if he would like some lunch. He said he was just about to make his first call to his office because he had forgotten about the three-hour time difference between Washington and Los Angeles and that I should go ahead because he didn't know how long he would be on the phone.

I told him that I would check with him later, hung up the phone, and sat there trying to think of somebody else in Washington who might like me to buy them lunch. Before I reached the bottom of my list the phone rang, and I found myself stuck with a luncheon date that I wasn't fast enough to lie my way out of.

It was Fastnaught, of course. I agreed to meet him in the hotel's restaurant at 12:30, and when I arrived he was already there, a martini on the table in front of him. I ordered a Scotch and water to keep him company, and after it came I let it sit there and waited to see how long it would take before he dived into his martini.

He held out for almost a minute, and his hand didn't shake very much at all as he lifted the drink to his lips. At least he didn't spill any. After a couple of swallows he put the glass back down and gave me a bleak little grin that he formed with only half of his mouth.

"I shake a little in the morning," he said.

"I noticed."

"I try to hold out until noon. Sometimes I don't always make it."

"You stash a bottle in your desk yet?"

He shook his head. "Not yet. I keep it in the car."

"Well, you're getting there."

"It looks that way, doesn't it?"

"Your wife drink?"

He nodded. "Like a trout. I figured it out last month. We must spend close to two fifty or three hundred on booze every month. It's about the same or maybe a little less than we spend on groceries."

"Any kids?"

He shook his head again. "She works. At least she does when she can get up in the morning, which is getting to be a problem."

"Cut out the booze and you could spend all that money on something else. A boat. Maybe a house in the country. Whatever you want."

"You make it sound simple."

"It's not simple. It's a matter of choice. The only drunks I ever knew who quit successfully were the ones who chose not to be drunks anymore. The choice they would've liked to have made, of course, was between being a gentleman drinker or a drunk. But they had run out of in-between. They could either be drunk or dry."

Fastnaught looked at me curiously. "You been there?" he said.

I picked up my drink and tasted it. It tasted the way it always did, of better times. Then I shook my head at Fastnaught's question. "I watched my old man when I was a kid. He was a college professor in Columbus. Associate professor, really. He went all the way down and then all the way back up. It took him about ten years. He liked to find the sleaziest bar possible, buy drinks for everybody, and then lecture them on *The Faerie Queene*. That was his specialty, Spenser. Then one night somebody brought him home with one of his eyes hanging down on his cheek. There was nobody home but me. I was thirteen, I think. I put the eye back in the socket. It seemed the thing to do. My mother was out of town. We sat there until four o'clock in the morning with him holding a wet washcloth over the eye that I'd put back. He didn't say a word. I didn't either. Then at four he said he thought that maybe I'd better call the doctor. Well, he lost the eye, but he never took another drink."

Fastnaught finished his martini and looked at me. "There's gotta be a moral there someplace."

"It helps if you're only thirteen."

"But you still put it away."

I nodded. "But I don't lecture in bars on *The Faerie Queene*."

"Huh," he said. "I think I know what you mean."

"I'm not sure that I do. You remember the man in the Hathaway shirt?"

"The guy with the patch over his eye?"

"He looked almost exactly like my old man, moustache and all, after my old man started wearing a black patch. For some reason I never bought a Hathaway shirt."

"Yeah," Fastnaught said. "I can see why. Or at least I think I can." He toyed with his empty glass. "You want another drink?"

"Sure," I said. "Why not?"

After the second round of drinks came, we ordered. Fastnaught decided to have an omelet. I chose the lamb stew, which the menu claimed was a house specialty.

As we waited for the food, Fastnaught leaned toward me over his drink. He looked almost as though he were crouched to spring.

"They're giving me a hard time," he said.

"I'm sorry to hear that," I said. "Who?"

"The FBI."

"How hard a time are they giving you?"

"They say they're being kept out of something that they oughta be in on."

"What did you say?"

"I told them that they were as much in on it as I am. But then I'm not in on it hardly at all, except that I didn't tell them that."

"They probably figured it out for themselves," I said.

"I had the Senator call them. I didn't wanta do that, and he sure as hell didn't want to, but he did anyhow. I've just about used him up on whatever he owes me. I was hoping to sort of save him for something else."

"Such as?"

"How the hell should I know?" Fastnaught said. "But the way I'm going, there's damn well gonna be something else that I could use him for. Probably to save my ass."

"How did he do?" I said. "With the FBI, I mean?"

Before Fastnaught could tell me, the waiter brought the omelet and the stew. I tasted the stew, and it was quite good. Fastnaught looked at his omelet as though it might wiggle. But after a moment he began to eat it, slowly.

"Why don't you have a bottle of beer to wash it down with?" I said.

Fastnaught looked at me coldly. "If I'da wanted a beer, I'd've ordered one." Then he thought about it for a moment and said, "Well, maybe I do want one."

After his beer came he ate some more of his omelet, perhaps a third, and then he put his knife and fork down. He looked at me. "He got us twenty-four hours."

"Who?"

"The Senator. He went all the way up to an assistant director and that's what he got us."

"What happens after twenty-four hours?"

"They jump in with both feet. Hard."

"I see."

"Well, what do you see?"

"What I see is that I can't see much difference. You've already jumped in hard. As long as they keep out of my way, I don't see how the FBI would matter. Some of them, if they don't take themselves too seriously, aren't all that bad."

"I thought I was doing you a favor," Fastnaught said.

"But having done it you want something in return, right?" I said.

"That's the way it works."

"No, it isn't. Not with me. What you want me to do is carry you around in my hip pocket. I don't work that way, and you know damn well I don't."

"When's it gonna be?" he said. "The switch, I mean. It's gonna be tonight, isn't it?"

"Sure," I said. "Tonight. Or is it tomorrow night, or maybe the day after? I forget."

Fastnaught shook his head. "It's tonight. You got wet shoes. That's how I know it's tonight."

"Jesus," I said.

"I'm a hell of a detective," he said. "There isn't a thing in God's world that would get you out in all this snow before noon today unless you had to go pick up the money. If you went to pick up the money, it means that you're ready to make the switch, except that you're not gonna do that in the middle of the five o'clock rush, so that means tonight."

"My word, Holmes."

"Yeah, I thought you'd like the wet shoes stuff,"

Fastnaught said. "It sort of helped, too, that I tailed you to the bank this morning. You and that other guy, what's his name?"

"Spivey."

"Uh-huh. Spivey. Max Spivey. He's big, isn't he?"

"Kind of," I said.

"Hell, I've been detecting all over the place this morning and me with the worst hangover a man ever had. I even did some more checking on this guy Jack Marsh. Guess what I found out?"

"How much is it going to cost me?"

Fastnaught grinned at me, and for a moment the grin took away most of the age and the lines that the liquor had written on his face. He looked very much like he did when I first knew him—young and merry and full of what-the-hell.

"Nothing," he said. "I'm gonna throw this one in free—except I'm gonna let you pay for the lunch."

"All right."

"I've been out to L.A. a couple of times on business and both times I worked with the same guy out there and we got to be pretty good drinking buddies. Well, this guy is a gossip merchant. I mean most cops are gossips, but this guy eats it. So I call him at home this morning just before I called you. Well, we go back and forth for a while—you know, the how the hell are you stuff and then I shoot him a couple of real juicy items about the White House and an L.A. congressman that I'd picked up somewhere, probably in the john at work. You know the kind of stuff you hear in this town."

"Uh-huh."

"Well, after that I ask him to tell me what he can about this guy Jack Marsh who I understand used to be with the cops out there before he went private. So this guy, this buddy of mine, tells me that almost everybody out there knows or at least has heard of Jack Marsh on account of he's so mean. Not that he's not good, my buddy says, in fact, he's probably the best private guy around out there, but he sure was one mean cop and from what my buddy hears he's even meaner now that he's gone private. My buddy says he doesn't know how Marsh was when he was in Army intelligence, but he was probably mean then too. He used to be a captain, Marsh, I mean."

"Who was he mean to?" I said.

"Well, there were a couple of Mexicans out there who probably thought he was mean, but they're not around anymore to tell about it."

"Dead?"

"Dead. It was a liquor store stickup and it could have gone either way, but my buddy says Marsh chose the other way. That was the first time. There were three more times before he quit and went private. It got so that guys didn't much want to work with him out there on account of he was so mean."

"But good?"

"Yeah, that's right, mean but good. Well, the other thing that my buddy hears is that Marsh is making a lot of money out there and that he's shacked up with this rich fox now that he's moved up in society. Well, guess who this rich fox is?"

I decided to spoil it for him. "Maude Goodwater. Except I don't think she's so rich anymore."

"But it's her book. I mean the one you're gonna buy back."

"That's right. It's her book. It used to be her father's."

"And she's shacked up with Jack Marsh."

"I think they call it living together nowadays. Maybe because it gives it a little more tone."

"Maybe," Fastnaught said. "Okay, she's living with mean Jack Marsh and she sends him here to Washington to pick up the book, but the next thing we know somebody's taken mean Jack out while he's got the book tucked under his arm and they're willing to sell it back and maybe mean Jack along with it for a quarter of a million. You like it?"

"Not much," I said.

"I sure as shit wouldn't like it if I was you," he said. "Maybe you'll like it even less when I drop the next little juicy item on you. And maybe you'll change your mind about having me in your hip pocket."

"Maybe," I said.

"Well, last month, my buddy tells me, a grand jury out there came within a cunt hair of handing down an indictment for extortion. Now guess who they were thinking of indicting?"

"Our Jack," I said.

"Yeah, our Jack," Fastnaught said. Something started working in his face and it spread to his eyes. They lost their dullness and took on a fresh, cold sparkle. "I've just had a flash," he said.

"And you're going to share it with me."

"You bet. You say this Goodwater broad is hard up?"

"That's what I understand. Although I'm not sure

what the rich think hard up is. I suppose it means that she's down to her last twenty or thirty thousand—something like that."

"So she decided to sell the book."

"That's right."

"For how much?"

"I don't know. At least half a million, from what Laws over at the Library of Congress tells me."

"Okay, let's see how this one fits. She and Marsh are sitting around out there in L.A. and she's crying because she's down to her last twenty or thirty thousand, like you say, and she's gonna have to sell the book just to scrape up half a million and Marsh comes up with this idea. Why doesn't she let him go pick it up? Then he'll just sort of disappear for a while and let everybody think he's been kidnapped along with the book. After that they'll call in some real honest go-between, who's not too bright, and he's got just the guy in mind, and they'll let the insurance company cut its losses and pay a quarter of a million to get the book back. What do you think, sugar? he says and she says, swell, honey, that's a wonderful idea, why don't you go ahead and set it up and we'll split. How do you like it, St. Ives?"

"It's got a lot of drama," I said. "There's one thing that bothers me."

"What?"

"What if I make the switch okay and get the book back?"

"Well?"

"Well, what if our Jack Marsh doesn't turn up until two days later when somebody finds him floating in the Anacostia?"

Fastnaught shook his head. "That isn't gonna happen."

"Can you guarantee it?"

I could see his mind working. Finally he said, "No, I can't guarantee it."

"Well, that's why you can't ride along in my hip pocket."

"No way, huh?"

"None."

He slumped back in his chair and looked at me with eyes that had lost the snap and sparkle they had had a few moments ago. They had gone dull again and old. The change made Fastnaught look tired and a little used up. "Well," he said, "the least you can do is buy me a brandy."

"I'll do better than that," I said. "I'll buy us both one."

-------------------- **EIGHT**

Right after I rented the Ford sedan from Hertz and bought a flashlight it began to snow again. It was about 3:30 in the afternoon and the snow had started coming down thick and steady and wet in a determined sort of way as though it had made up its mind to cover everything up at least twelve inches deep even if it took all afternoon and the rest of the night.

According to the radio the federal government had made up its mind a little more quickly this time. It had decided to let all of its employees go home at four and I got caught in that traffic and it wasn't until five that I got back to the hotel.

I checked with the desk to see whether there were any messages. There weren't so I used a house phone to call Max Spivey. "I'm downstairs," I told him. "Because of this weather and one other thing maybe you'd better turn the money over to me now."

"I'll be right down," he said.

I waited for him at the elevator and after he got there we went over to the desk and Spivey asked for and was given the suitcase. Before he handed it to me he said, "You mentioned one other thing."

I nodded. "There's a Washington cop who wants me to take him with me. I don't want to, so I may have to leave early to make sure that he's not tagging along. Also I don't know what this snow will do. It may make them want to move the switch up to an earlier time. If they do, it could be pretty short notice so I thought I'd better get the money now."

"It's all yours," he said and handed the suitcase over.

"I'll sign something if you want me to."

He shook his head. "No need. You want to have dinner?"

"I'd better stick by the phone in case they call. I'll have something sent up."

"Anything else I can do?" he said.

"I can't think of anything. I'll check with you before I leave. Will you be in your room?"

He nodded.

"Okay. Then I'll go on up."

Spivey said he wanted to pick up something to read so I rode the elevator up alone. Once inside the room I locked and bolted the door and put the money in the closet. After that I ran some water into the tub as hot as I could stand it, eased down into it, and thought about the absurdity of my calling. I decided that if it were nothing else, it was good experience. I could always get a job as a Western Union messenger, providing that Western Union still used messengers, which I wasn't at all sure that it did. I tried to remember the last time that a messenger had delivered a telegram to me and what his uniform had looked like, but I couldn't. By then the water had grown cool so I got out of the tub, dried off, got dressed, and turned on the television set. It was time for the evening network news and I watched Walter Cronkite, as avuncular as ever, reduce complicated stories to twenty-five oversimplified words or less.

When the news was over I called room service and ordered a roast beef sandwich, a glass of milk, and a pot of coffee. When they came I sat there and ate and watched some more television and thought about nothing other than how awful it was and always is.

At ten I rose, went over to the window, and looked out. It was still snowing as hard or perhaps even harder than before. I turned, picked up the phone, and called Max Spivey. After he answered, I said, "This is St. Ives. I'm leaving."

"Aren't you a little early?"

"I don't think so," I said. "Not with this weather."

"Well, hell, all I can say is good luck."

"I'll check with you when I get back."

"Do that," he said.

The car was in a garage a block away. When I had left New York I hadn't counted on snow and all I had was a light topcoat. I put it on, turned the collar up, took the suitcase out of the closet, and rode the elevator down to the lobby. The doorman was standing outside watching the snow come down.

"Any chance for a cab?" I said.

He shook his head. "There hasn't been one out there in an hour."

I looked around the lobby. It was deserted except for the hotel staff. I clutched the collar of my topcoat, ducked my head, and went out into the snow.

I suppose that it was as close to a blizzard as Washington gets. A wind had come up out of the north and drove the flakes into my face as I walked up Sixteenth Street. I could see a yard in front of me, possibly two. I looked back a couple of times but there was nothing to see but more snow. There seemed to be almost no cars in the street.

By the time I got to the garage I was half frozen. I took my topcoat off and shook it to remove the snow. When I gave the black attendant my parking ticket he said, "You ain't goin' out in this shit, are ya?"

"I'm a doctor," I said.

He went off to get the Ford. I could hear him start the engine and then there was a clicking sound which was the chains that I had ordered put on when I rented it. The attendant pulled the car up in front of me and got out. I gave him fifty cents, reached in and got the keys, cutting off the engine. I went back and unlocked the trunk and put the suitcase in it and slammed down the lid.

The attendant was still hanging around when I got in the car. "You gotta operate tonight?" he said.

I nodded. "Brain tumor."

"Jesus," he said.

I don't know why I bothered to lie to him. Perhaps because the reason that I gave for my going out into that snow made us both feel better. At least it made sense.

I turned left and drove down I Street until I came

to Fifteenth. I turned left again, crossed K, and drove past the Washington Post and the Madison hotel. I drove slowly, not more than fifteen or twenty. There was almost no traffic except for an occasional police cruiser. It was half past ten and Washington apparently had gone to bed early. It usually holds out until eleven.

On the other side of Massachusetts Avenue, Fifteenth Street became one way and I pulled over into the left lane. The windshield wipers were doing a good job of getting rid of most of the snow and the rear window was being kept fairly clear by its heating element.

I turned left on R Street, which was also one way, drove a block, and pulled over to the curb. A car went past me and disappeared into the snow. I started up again, found a driveway, turned into it, and backed out, now going the wrong way on R Street. I drove slowly and carefully until I reached Fifteenth again and then turned left. There was no traffic, at least none I could see.

After that I drove aimlessly, turning left and then right after every few blocks. By a quarter to eleven I found myself on Wisconsin Avenue in Georgetown. On the left was a hamburger place that had tables at its window. I parked the car and went in.

It was one of those places that are self-service. I got a cup of coffee and carried it over to one of the window tables. There was nobody in the place except for the two kids who ran it and who kept arguing with each other about how soon they could close up and go home.

I sat there for three-quarters of an hour and drank three cups of coffee. A few cars went by outside, but not many. There were almost no pedestrians. I checked the city map that the Hertz people had given me and figured out my route. At 11:30 I went out, brushed the snow off the windshield and got back into the car.

It was snowing even harder than before. I drove east on M Street through Georgetown until I came to Twenty-third Street and turned south. I kept driving, went around a traffic circle, and on past the State Department until I came to the Lincoln Memorial. After I went around the memorial Twenty-third Street was supposed to turn into something called Ohio Drive. I found it, or hoped that I did, and after crossing a small bridge I drove for another five minutes. I looked at my watch. It was six minutes until twelve. I stopped the car and waited four minutes. Then I drove slowly on for two minutes more until Ohio Drive started to bend sharply left, which meant that I was where I was supposed to be, at Haines Point. I saw the car a moment later. It was parked and its lights were off. It should have been a green or a blue Chevrolet, but because of the snow I couldn't be sure. I decided that it would have to do. I stopped my own car, put it in reverse, and backed up slowly until I was what I hoped was fifty feet away. I looked at my watch. It was exactly midnight.

I switched off the Ford's headlights, remembered the flashlight that I had bought earlier, took it out of the glove compartment, got out of the car, went around to the rear, and opened the trunk. I stood there and listened. I'm not sure what I was listening for because there was nothing to hear other than my own breathing.

I took the suitcase out of the trunk and started walking toward the car that was supposed to be a green or a blue Chevrolet. The snow came well over my ankles and I wondered whether the car up ahead had chains or snow tires.

I had switched the flashlight on and its beam picked up the car. It was about fifteen feet ahead. When I reached it I put the suitcase down on my right so that I could open the trunk. The trunk was locked. I remember saying, "Shit," and then there was a sudden movement on my right. It was only a blur, but I ducked and something cold and hard slammed into my neck just below my right ear. If I hadn't ducked, it would have slammed into my temple.

I remember that I sat down in the snow. I sat down in it because I could no longer stand up. I watched an ungloved hand pick up the suitcase. I tried to see who the hand belonged to, but I couldn't make him out because he had already turned. The engine of the car started and I watched the back door open. The suitcase disappeared inside the car and the back door slammed shut. I decided it was time to get up and say something, perhaps something such as, "You can't do that," or "What the hell's going on here?"

Somebody else said something instead. A voice said, "Hold it right there, police!" The figure by the car hesitated, but just for a moment. Then he had the front door open and he was getting in, or starting to, and then there was the shot. The first shot must have caught him in the back because he arced backward and then stumbled forward toward the car. Its door was still open and he was still determined to get into it. He might have made it except that the car started moving away. He tried to throw himself into the moving car, but there was a second shot that caught him and spun him around until he was facing me and I wondered how I could see him so clearly in all that snow and dark until I noticed that I was still holding the flashlight. He went down on his knees first, not three feet away from me, and stayed that way for a moment. His mouth worked a couple of times, as if he were talking to himself, perhaps about his rotten luck. Then he pitched forward into the snow and lay still.

I sat there and stared at him for a moment. Then I noticed that his face was buried in the snow. I bent forward and tugged at him until I got his head turned around so that he could breathe. I needn't have bothered.

A voice to my right and behind me said, "You all right?"

"Oh hell, yes," I said. "I just like to sit in the snow."

It was Fastnaught. He knelt down near my feet and touched his fingers to the man's neck. He held them there for what seemed to be a long time.

"I guess he's dead," Fastnaught said.

"You guess?"

"He's dead."

I decided to move my head. I turned it to the left and it felt all right. Then I turned it to the right. That was a mistake. A sharp pain tore through it and made me gasp. I touched my neck just below my right ear. There was a pronounced swelling but nothing seemed broken or cracked. I found that if I held my head just so, bent slightly to the right, the pain wasn't so bad. It also must have made me look a little odd because Fastnaught said, "What's the matter with you? I thought you said you were okay."

"It's nothing," I said. "Just a broken neck."

"You know him?"

"Who?"

"Him. There."

"Oh, you mean the guy you shot. The one there at my feet in the snow. That one. No, I don't think we've met. Since you shot him, I thought you probably must know him."

"You're babbling," Fastnaught said. "You better get up out of that snow."

I got up, or started to, and then sat back down. Things had started to grow dim. I picked up a handful of snow and smeared it over my face. The shock of the cold made me start to shake.

"You got the trembles," Fastnaught said.

"Is that what they're called?"

"You better let me help you up."

He helped me up. I stood there for a moment and continued to shake with cold or shock or both. Fastnaught said, "Give me that," and took the flashlight. He shined it in my face. "You sure nothing's busted?"

"I don't think so," I said.

"How come you're holding your head like that?"

"It's what's called a faintly quizzical angle," I said. "People in books do it a lot."

"It looks silly."

"Maybe that's because I've got a lot of silly questions for you."

"Later," Fastnaught said. He knelt down and started going through the dead man's pockets using the flashlight to examine what he found. Some of the light splashed over the man's face. It was a fairly young face which now would never reach middle age. The grey eyes were still open and snow had fallen into them and melted, which made them appear to be full of tears. But tears didn't go with that face. Even dead it had a smart, clever look to it with a thin, tight mouth and a sharp nose and a tough, biggish chin. It was a hard face, I decided, and the last time that those grey eyes had been wet with tears must have been thirty years ago when the dead man was six or possibly seven.

Fastnaught grunted and stood up. He held a thin black wallet under the flashlight. "Well, guess who we got here?" he said.

"My first guess," I said, "is going to be Jack Marsh, late of Los Angeles."

"Huh," he said. "You figured it out. My theory about Marsh was pretty good, wasn't it?"

"It was wonderful," I said. "Even brilliant. And now I'm sure you're going to tell me, just before I freeze to death, who drove off in that car with a quarter of a million dollars."

"They got the money?" he said. "Shit. I didn't see that. I saw you go down and that's when I shot at him. But I didn't see him get the money."

"He threw it into the back seat," I said. "I was to give them the money and get the book, but it didn't work out like that. He threw the money into the back seat and then you shot him and then the car drove off with all that money without bothering to leave the book unless it's somewhere over there in the snow."

"Wait a minute," Fastnaught said. He moved over to where the car had been parked and shined the flashlight around. He bent over and picked up something and came back to where I stood. "No book," he said.

"Somehow I didn't think there would be."

"But I found this," he said and held it out for me to look at. It was an automatic pistol. I thought that it looked like a Colt .38, but I wasn't sure. I decided that it really didn't matter.

"That's a great help."

"It is to me," he said.

"It gets you off, doesn't it?"

"Yeah. They don't like us just to go around shooting just anybody. They like 'em to be either armed or dangerous or both. And that's what he was, wasn't he, St. Ives? Armed and dangerous."

"I didn't see any gun," I said.

"You felt it. That's just as good."

"I'm freezing," I said.

"Let's go get in my car. I got a bottle in there. You can suck on it while I call this thing in."

Fastnaught's car was parked twenty or thirty feet behind mine. When we were inside he started the engine and switched the heater on full blast. Then he used his radio to talk over, but I didn't listen to him. I was busy drinking his whiskey.

When he was through with the radio he reached for the bottle. "You gave me quite a little ride tonight," he said. "I nearly froze my ass off. Backing up and going the wrong way on R Street. That was cute."

"I thought so."

"You woulda lost me if it hadn't been for the snow. In snow you can stick real close to somebody with your lights off and they can't even tell."

"I'll remember that next time," I said.

"You think there's gonna be a next time?"

"Why not?"

"Well, you sorta fucked this thing up, didn't you? You lost the money. You didn't get the book back. I don't know, but if I was looking for a go-between in the Yellow Pages, I think maybe you'd be about the last one I'd call."

"I guess I'll have to learn to live with it."

Fastnaught tipped the bottle up and took another drink. "Now me on the other hand, I'm sittin' sorta pretty. I got Jack Marsh out there in the snow. That's half of it. I figure I can pull in the other half without too much sweat. It might take a little trip but I figure they'll go for it now."

"A little trip where?" I said.

"Out to Los Angeles." He turned in the seat and I could feel him looking at me. "Knowing you, maybe I'll see you out there."

"No," I said. "I don't think you will."

──────────────────── NINE

The police arrived in a swarm of blue and white cars. There must have been six or seven units not counting an ambulance. After they were through figuring out what had happened they sent me over to George Washington University Hospital in the company of two very young uniformed policemen.

A pair of equally young doctors who were working the emergency room that night turned my head this way and that, took some X rays, cracked a couple of jokes, and gave me a small brown packet of pills.

"You're going to have a hell of a stiff neck for a few days," one of them said. "These might help a little."

"What are they?"

"Muscle relaxants."

"Nothing's broken though?" I said.

"Not even cracked."

The two young policemen took me down to headquarters on Indiana Avenue where they handed me over to a pair of homicide detectives who took turns asking questions for nearly an hour. After they were through I signed a statement that one of them typed up. By then it was a little after two o'clock.

"Wait here," one of the homicide detectives said. "I'll go see if I can find somebody to run you back to your hotel."

He was gone quite a long time, at least a quarter of an hour. I sat there in the hard grey metal chair and waited. People wandered in, most of them men with pistols on their belts. Some of them looked at me, but there was little curiosity in their glances. I was just somebody else who had brushed up against violent death, and that was nothing to get excited about. Violent death was their business.

When the homicide detective came back Fastnaught was with him. "Okay, Mr. St. Ives," the detective said. "You can go now. Lieutenant Fastnaught here will drop you by your hotel."

"Anything else?" I said.

"Not now."

"If there is, I'll be in New York."

He stared at me suspiciously. It was probably the only way he knew how to stare. "I know where you'll be," he said.

Fastnaught touched my arm. "Let's go."

I followed him out to the elevator. By the time it came, Fastnaught was humming to himself. I couldn't make out the tune because he didn't hum very well. He was still humming when we got into his car and he took the fifth from the glove compartment. He stopped humming long enough to put the bottle to his lips and take a deep swallow.

"You want a drink?" he said.

I shook my head. "They liked it, huh?"

"What?"

"Your story."

"Oh, yeah. That. They liked it just fine. They liked it even better after they sent a couple of guys over to your hotel to talk to Max Spivey. I'm not gonna get any commendation, but with what you told 'em and with what Max Spivey told 'em, I came up smelling like that rose they keep talking about. You've gotta talk to Spivey now, don't you?"

"That's right."

"From what I hear, he's not too happy."

"No. I suppose he's not."

"You gonna talk to him tonight?"

"Yes."

"What're you gonna tell him?"

"I'm going to tell him my version of what happened."

"You wanta know what I would do if I was you, after I got through telling him that?"

"What?"

"Duck."

After he got through chuckling over that, Fastnaught took one more drink, put the bottle back in the glove compartment, and started the engine. He was humming to himself again as he drove me back to the Hay Adams. It had stopped snowing by then and here and there a few street-cleaning crews were out. They looked cold and discouraged.

"They're gonna put me on administrative leave, you know," Fastnaught said as he turned down Sixteenth Street.

"They are?"

"It'll look better that way. I told 'em I could use a couple of weeks of it while they got everything cleared up."

"That'll give you more time to spend with your wife, won't it?"

Fastnaught looked at me. "You're funny, St. Ives. You know that, you're funny as hell."

"Sure."

He pulled up into the driveway that runs in front of the entrance to the Hay Adams. I looked at my watch. It was nearly a quarter to three. I wanted to get out of the car and go into the hotel and up to my room where it was warm and quiet and where nobody wanted to ask me any more questions about how stupid or careless I had been. I very much wanted to be alone, but Fastnaught needed to talk some more. Or maybe the liquor did.

"Two weeks," he said. "That oughta be enough."

"Plenty of time," I said.

"Yeah, two weeks from now, maybe right about this time, I might be giving you a call. You be in New York?"

"That's right. New York."

"You in the book?"

"Yes."

"Well, don't be surprised if I give you a ring about then."

"What're we going to talk about?"

"We don't have to talk about anything. I'll just tell you who he is."

"Who?"

"The other guy. The one who drove off in the car tonight with all the money."

"Oh," I said. "Him."

"What's the matter, don't you wanta know who he is?"

"Look, I've had a long night. My neck hurts and so does my pride. I don't know which hurts more. But it's not doing either of them any good to sit here and listen to you or the booze, or maybe both, tell me how clever you're going to be two weeks from now. For me, it's over. I'm out of it."

I was halfway out of the car when Fastnaught spoke. I turned to look at him. The booze had gone from both his voice and his eyes. His voice had a snap to it and his eyes were bright and hard and somehow cunning.

"Let me tell you something, St. Ives."

"All right."

"I'm going to find him."

"Fine. I wish you luck."

"No you don't. What you're hoping is that I'll stumble around and make a mess of it. That's what you're really hoping, isn't it?"

I shrugged. "I'm not sure. Maybe."

He nodded as if my answer satisfied him. "Let me ask you something else," he said. "Have you ever thought of maybe going into some other line of work?"

"That very thought occurred to me only tonight," I said, got out of the car, and closed the car door without quite slamming it. Fastnaught nodded and waved at me as he drove off. He was probably humming again.

Max Spivey was half dressed. I couldn't tell whether

he had been on his way to bed when he stopped taking off his clothes or whether he had been rudely awakened and just pulled on whatever was available. He had on a tee shirt and a pair of pants and socks. The tee shirt had a small hole in it down near the waist. His beard was heavy and his hair was damp and rumpled as though he had had time to shower, but not to shave. He didn't smile when he opened the door to my knock.

"You look awful," he said.

"Then I look like I feel."

"You got slugged? That's what the cops said."

"By your good friend."

Something moved across Spivey's face, something like pain or regret or perhaps even guilt. "Funny," he said. "I should be mad as hell at Jack and I guess I am a little. But mostly all I can feel is sorry that he's dead. The son of a bitch."

"There was somebody in it with him," I said. "Have you got any ideas?"

"The cops told me," Spivey said. "I've been thinking about it. In fact, I haven't been thinking about anything else. Jack knew a lot of people and a lot of them were bent all out of shape. Any number of them would have jumped at a chance like this." He stared at me curiously. "You want to sit down? You don't look so good."

"Maybe I'd better," I said. I sat down on a chair near the writing desk.

"What about a drink?" he said. "I've got some Scotch and some ice. I don't think it's all melted yet."

"Thanks," I said.

He poured two drinks, mixed them with water from

the tap in the bathroom, and handed me one. "I heard what the cops had to say," he said. "What's your version?"

I told him my version and when I was through, Spivey had some questions. Some very good questions.

"You say the car trunk was locked?"

"That's right."

"Then it wasn't because they panicked or anything like that, was it?"

"No."

"I mean they never intended to come up with the book."

"It looks that way."

"The money. The money bothers me. It bothers me quite a lot."

I nodded. "I can imagine."

"After you were slugged, you were sitting down in the snow. Right?"

"That's right."

"Now are you absolutely sure that you saw Marsh throw the suitcase into the car?"

"I'm sure," I said. "He threw it into the back seat."

"What about this lieutenant, what's his name—uh—"

"Fastnaught," I said.

"Yeah, Fastnaught. That was an awful lot of money being tossed around. You had just been slugged hard, very hard, I'd say from the size of that lump under your ear. Are you sure you didn't black out for maybe five or ten seconds?"

"You mean just long enough for Fastnaught to somehow get his hands on the money?"

Spivey shrugged. "It's a possibility."

"There's an even better one," I said. "A quarter of a million dollars is an awful lot of money. Let's say I've known Fastnaught for a while and so we get together and decide to go for it. In this version, Jack Marsh is all by himself. We go through with it just like it was set up, except that when Marsh gets out of the car Fastnaught blows him in two. Then to make it look good, Fastnaught bangs me on the neck, but not too hard, and we dump Marsh's car somewhere, tuck the money away safe, and call in the cops. How do you like that possibility?"

"It's not the first time that it's been entertained tonight," Spivey said. "When the cops come to see me they brought it up, but only as a possibility."

"The snow," I said.

He nodded. "That's right, the snow. If it hadn't been for the snow, I think they might still be working on it, but the car tracks didn't fit. If you had dumped Marsh's car someplace, that means you would have had to come back and that would have meant another set of car tracks. There weren't any."

"We could have walked," I said.

"They checked that out, too," he said. "You didn't walk."

"So that means that somebody somewhere in this town has got a quarter of a million in a suitcase and an old book. The book bothers me."

"It bothers the hell out of me," Spivey said. "If I don't get it back, it means we're out seven hundred and fifty thousand bucks—not just a quarter of a million."

"You mean the insurance. You'll still have to pay off Maude Goodwater."

"That's right."

"Does she know yet?"

"You mean about what happened tonight?"

I nodded.

"Yeah, I called her earlier while the cops were here. They talked to her, too. She took it hard—about Jack Marsh, I mean."

"Fastnaught has another theory," I said. "He thinks she might have been in on it from the start."

"Maude?"

I nodded. "Maude."

He shook his head. "Jack—well, yes. Jack's maybe my fault and maybe he's Maude's fault a little, too. It was a big score—a quarter of a million dollars and Jack probably needed the money. He always needed money. But Maude—" He shook his head and didn't bother with the rest of the sentence.

"Why not Maude?" I said.

He thought about it for a moment. "Probably because she's just too honest."

"That's one reason," I said. "It's probably as good as any and better than most. But it still leaves the book."

Spivey put his drink down, clasped his hands behind his neck, and gave himself a tremendous stretch that made his chest bulge out until it threatened to fill half the room. I wondered what his chest was fully expanded—at least fifty-five inches. Maybe even more. When he was through stretching, he said, "I wonder what a hot copy of Pliny's *Historia Naturalis* would bring?"

"They wouldn't take that kind of a chance," I said.

"Then why go to all that trouble, if they're not

going to peddle it? Why didn't they just ransom it back?"

"Maybe the only reason they won't go around trying to peddle it is that they don't have to. Maybe they already have their buyer."

Spivey got up quickly and started pacing. The room wasn't large enough for him to do a proper job of it so he settled for three strides one way and then three strides back. He ground his right fist into his left hand as he paced. I don't think he knew that he was doing it. If he had, it would have been a little theatrical. "Yeah," he said. "That makes it work. Otherwise it wouldn't." He spun around and pointed a big forefinger at me. "Jack could have dug him up. A buyer, I mean. He would've known where to find one. Or who to go to, anyway. Maybe a middleman."

I yawned. I couldn't help it. "You'll be looking for a nut," I said. "Or maybe only an eccentric. But there's one thing you can be sure of about him."

"What?"

"He'll be rich. Very, very rich."

Spivey started pacing again. I watched as he used three paces to cover twelve feet one way and then back again just like before. He must have traveled the equivalent of a couple of blocks before he stopped again, whirled around, and once more aimed his huge forefinger at me like a pistol.

"You fucked up, St. Ives."

"I was wondering when you were going to get around to it. I've been thinking about it and you're right, I did fuck up. If I'd worked at it a little harder, I should've been able to shake Fastnaught. And if I'd lost him, then

Jack Marsh would still be alive, but you'd still be out a quarter of a million dollars—and the book."

"The switch," Spivey said. "You could have set that up better."

I shook my head. "The switch is always the thief's option. Sometimes you can refine it, but you can't originate it because he'll smell double cross and probably refuse to deal. So all you can do is work within the framework of what he sets up and take your chances. And that's what I get paid for, taking those chances."

"Did you ever have one go sour like this before?" Spivey said.

I nodded. "A few times. Once it was an African shield. Another time it was an old sword in London."

"What did you do?"

"What do you mean, what did I do?"

Spivey made an impatient gesture. "I mean did you just drop it or did you try to do something about it?"

"Sometimes I messed around a little."

He nodded. "And after you got through messing around, what did you have?"

"Some answers. That's about all."

"A deal," Spivey said.

"What kind of a deal?"

"You're out twenty-five thousand dollars, right?"

"Plus my pride."

"Yeah, your pride. I almost forgot about that. You come up with the answers on this one—all the answers—and Pacifica insurances will pay you twenty-five thousand. You come up with some answers that lead to our recovering both the book and the quarter of a million, and we'll go ten percent of everything."

"That's seventy-five thousand."

"A lot of money."

"You could hire a bunch of guys for that—guys with licenses that they hang on their walls. I'm not a private investigator."

"I'll put some private guys on it," Spivey said. "I'll have to. And probably all they'll come up with is their bill. You—you're my outside chance and you don't cost anything unless you produce."

"Expenses," I said.

Spivey shook his head. "Not even expenses."

"I'll tell you what I'll do."

"What?"

"I'll think about it."

TEN

Dr. Ogletree didn't have any clothes on, which was all right with me because Dr. Ogletree was not quite thirty, not quite five-foot-one, and not quite as blond all over as the tight golden curls on her head would have one assume.

Dr. Mary Frances Ogletree was a nice Southern girl, from Sylacauga, Alabama, to be exact, who even now, at twenty-nine, looked as though she might very well be out there on a crisp autumn afternoon in short skirt and sweater, turning handsprings every time the Crimson Tide crunched through with another six points against Ole Miss or Tennessee or whoever it is that Alabama plays.

Although she still looked like a cheerleader, Dr. Ogletree was actually a much respected psychiatrist who specialized in autistic children. I thought that she was a little young to be a psychiatrist until I learned that she had been graduated from high school at fifteen, from college at eighteen, and from medical school at twenty-three. When I had met her six months ago I also thought that she was a bit young to be doing what she was doing just then, which was gutting me with three queens in a stud game up at Joe Awful's place on One Hundred and Nineteenth Street in Harlem, which isn't exactly where one would expect to run into a nice Southern girl.

Joe Awful's name wasn't really Awful, it was Joe Ophelle, and he had once played pro basketball a long time ago. He now gambled for a living and was quite good at it. His youngest daughter was a patient of Dr. Ogletree's, which was how she had come to be invited, although the invitation had been Joe Awful's idea of a pleasant little joke.

His little joke had cost him $1,400 that night and it had cost me $900. I had offered to see Dr. Ogletree home, providing that she paid for the taxi since I couldn't because she had just won my last dime. She had not only paid for the taxi, but she also had bought our breakfast at an all-night coffee shop on East Seventy-third, about a block from her apartment, which was where I now watched her as she tiptoed around in search of some cigarettes.

"We really should quit off our cigarette habit," she said as she came back with a package of Lucky Strikes and sat down cross-legged on the bed.

"My list of don'ts is already too long," I said.

"You want to know what the biggest bad habit I ever shucked was?"

"What?"

"The South."

"You didn't get rid of it, you just left it. You still talk as though you have a mouthful of hot grits."

"Actually, Mr. St. Ives, I can talk in virtually any manner that I choose," she said, doing a rather good Mayfair accent.

"That's because you're a mimic and that's not talent, it's a gift."

"When I say I shucked off the South I mean I got rid of the bad parts. I hung on tight to the good parts."

"What good parts?"

"Manners, acquired sociability, natural sympathetic concern, stuff like that. Some of it was real and some of it was artificial, but what I liked I kept. I don't know whether it's still there like it was when I was growing up and learning it all from my grandmother. You have to learn it, you know. She used to say that the new wave of discrimination would be aimed at the gently born."

"I thought your father was a riverboat gambler. That's not exactly what I'd call quality folks."

She shook her head and smiled. "There weren't any real riverboats left or he would have been. I just tell some people that. He gambled his way through Princeton, then through the Army Air Corps, and then through what was left of a very short but one hell of a merry life. He and my mother died in a car wreck outside of Miami when I was seven, but by then he had already taught me a profession—card-gaming, as he called it. God, he was good. I've talked to people who played with him. He was a natural gambler. There aren't many of them, you know."

"What's the composition of one?" I said. "I mean, if you were speaking professionally."

She thought about it a while. "Almost total self acceptance. That's one. You combine that with an almost complete lack of guilt, throw in a good mind, an inclination toward risk-taking, and you come up with a successful gambler—or almost a successful anything else, except possibly a poet. You could almost gamble for a living, you know."

"I've thought of it."

She shook her head and ran her finger down my bare chest until it tickled. "Don't try it, sugarplum. Not for a living anyhow. You couldn't stand the guilt."

"I don't mind losing once in a while."

"You wouldn't feel guilty about losing," she said. "It's the winning that would be your problem. You wouldn't ever be quite sure that you deserved it."

I thought about that for a moment. "Maybe I should turn poet."

"Why don't you just stay what you are—gentleman go-between and awfully good screw."

"That thing I was on down in Washington."

"Last week?"

"Uh-huh. Last week. It didn't turn out too well."

She nodded. "I could tell."

"How?"

"A mild hesitancy here and there. It would take a trained eye to notice it." She grinned. "Or a trained body."

"I'm thinking about giving it another shot."

"Can you?" she said. "I mean, can you pick it up and screw it back together?"

"I don't know."

"Do you want to?"

"Uh-huh. I think so."

"But what?"

"It might be messy."

"How messy?"

"I'm not sure. One guy's already been killed. If I stir things up some more, it might get nasty."

"For you?"

"There's a chance, but there always is with that much money involved."

"When did you get back from Washington?"

"Thursday."

"And today's Sunday. What've you been doing, sitting up there in that cave of yours, throwing rocks at the lions and tigers?"

"Something like that."

"All by yourself, of course."

"I had a little gin for company."

"And when you couldn't stand you and the gin anymore, you called me and came over here to make sure that what you've already made up your mind to do is really just one hell of a good idea. That's what you'd like me to tell you, isn't it? Except you'd like it to be frosted over with a little professional jargon."

"When I want advice, I can always read some tea leaves."

"All right, reassurance then. What's wrong with wanting reassurance? I don't mind people telling me I'm wonderful. That's because I don't mind thinking I'm pretty wonderful myself."

"You're pretty wonderful all right, Mary Frances."

"See, I didn't even blush although I could've if I'd wanted to. My grandmother taught me how. She said it was most becoming of well brought up young ladies to be able to blush, even when they didn't feel like it. She taught me a lot of crap like that."

"Well, doctor, you certainly have been a help. I don't know what I would've done without you."

"I know what you would've done," she said with another grin.

"What?"

"You'd have found somebody else to play doctor with."

We decided that we were hungry so we took a shower together, which was pleasant, and then got dressed. It took Mary Frances longer so I wandered around her apartment, lifted up the tops of jars and peered inside, read the titles of some of the books that covered two walls of her living room, studied a couple of paintings that she had recently bought, and snooped around her desk, but resisted reading her mail.

It was an apartment whose furnishings had been selected with a great deal of care and thought, but managed to look as though they had come together by happy chance. There was a pale green sofa and a scarlet easy chair that shouldn't have gone together at all, but did. There were some low polished tables and some plump pillows and some more chairs and in one corner was a small piano that Mary Frances liked to play while she sang revolutionary songs. Any revolution would do and sometimes I joined in with her on the chorus of "Marching Through Georgia," although we sometimes argued about whether it qualified.

When she came out of the bedroom she was wearing a pair of light tan pants, a short, dark suede jacket over

111

a dark green blouse, and a big floppy hat which, by rights, she was too short to wear, but which on her looked just right.

"You look as good with your clothes on as you do with them off, which is smashing," I said.

She made a mock curtsy. "You do turn a wicked compliment, sir," she said. "And I thank you."

"I was just wondering."

"About what?"

"About whether there might be a vacancy in this building. I'm being evicted."

"Now that's the best goddamn news I've heard since Easter week. When?"

"End of the month."

"And you haven't found any place yet?"

"I haven't even looked."

"You should have got out of that hole you live in years ago."

"Probably. There was a small matter of inertia."

She stood in front of me, her small fists on her hips. "I've just had one hell of a good idea."

"What?"

"You can move in here."

I looked around the room. "That's a very kind offer."

"That's not an offer. It's a proposition. We'll split the rent and everything else right down the line. If it doesn't work out, then you can pack up and move on. But it'll work. I don't know whether I'm in love with you, St. Ives, but I'm damned fond of you and the rest of it—well, hell, we'll work at it."

"You're pretty sure, aren't you?" I said.

"Well, aren't you?"

"Maybe."

"What's the matter, then? Does it burn you because I asked you instead of you asking me?"

"I think we're both a bit beyond that. It's just that if I move in, I don't want to move out."

"That's fair enough. I sort of like that."

I put my arms around her and held her close. Then I tipped her face up to mine and kissed her.

"I'm going to have to be gone for a while," I said.

"On this thing we were talking about?"

"Yes."

"How long?"

"A week. That's all I'll give it."

"Where?"

"Los Angeles."

"When do you think you'll make up your mind about my proposition?"

"Give me a couple of days. Maybe three. I'll call you."

"You're leaving when, tomorrow?"

"Yes."

"Okay. Call me and tell me yes, no, or maybe. I'm shameless. I'll even settle for maybe."

"It won't be maybe," I said.

"Phil."

"What?"

"You'd be a fool to say no."

"Yes," I said. "I know."

-------------------- **ELEVEN**

I made four calls late that Sunday night. The first call was to Max Spivey out in Los Angeles to tell him that I would be there the next day. The second call was to Myron Greene in Darien to let him know what I had decided to do. The third call was to United Airlines for a reservation, and the fourth call was to Mickey Cupini who lived in Brooklyn, but who ran his union out of offices down near City Hall. He was the executive director of a public employees' council that embraced nearly all the unionized city workers with the exception of the cops and the firemen and some hospital workers. He ran it as a despot would run it and every once in a while, just to show his muscle, he would call out the garbage collectors or the bridge tenders or the welfare workers and the city would gasp and go into a rapid decline until Cupini got what he wanted.

He was also a power in the Democratic Party, could make his weight felt down in Washington, and maintained loose but cordial relations with organized crime among whose more notorious middle-management members he could count three cousins and one brother-in-law.

Mickey Cupini was smart, articulate, fairly ruthless, and had once confessed to me that by the time he was fifty-five he intended to be president of the AFL-CIO. He still had twenty years to go and I felt that he might very well make it. Fifteen years ago when he had been a kid head-merchant, struggling to organize the city's white collar workers who then thought of themselves as belonging more to management than to labor, I had written him up in a couple of more or less sympathetic columns. He had never forgotten it and every Christmas thereafter, he had sent me a twenty-pound turkey, which I usually turned over to an aging gay couple who lived on the fifth floor of the Adelphi, were marvelous cooks, and didn't have too much money.

When I was through asking Mickey Cupini about his wife and each of his six kids, I asked if he would like to have lunch the next day. He said that he would and we agreed to meet at Minuto's, which is a small restaurant down on Eighteenth Street where the food would be good and the service even better, possibly because it was owned by Mickey Cupini's wife's cousin.

Cupini was already there when I arrived at one o'clock the next day with my suitcase.

"You going out of town?" he said after we shook hands.

"For a few days," I said.

There were only eight tables and four booths in Minuto's and it was packed as always with reservations running right up until two o'clock. Cupini and I had the back booth and I let him order for me because he liked to make a little ceremony out of it.

"You haven't been around lately," Cupini said when he was through ordering. "What've you been up to?"

"Not a hell of a lot," I said.

"You married again?"

"No."

"Got a girl?"

"Well, there's this one I've been seeing a lot of."

Cupini nodded several times. "That's good. You oughta get married and if you don't get married, you oughta move in with her. Living alone's what's bad."

"How's the labor business?" I said.

Cupini shook his head. "The fuckin' city's going broke. The fuckin' mayor wants to fire everybody. The fuckin' members are screamin' for more dough. Outside of that, business is swell."

"I'm going out to L.A. today, Mickey."

"Uh-huh." There was nothing in the "uh-huh" one way or another. It was a cautious acknowledgment that I was going to ask a favor that he wasn't sure he could grant. Or would want to.

"How're you fixed out in L.A.?"

"Pretty good. We got about forty percent of the city and county employees and we're moving up."

"Any of them broke or out of work?"

"What'd you have in mind?"

"I'm going to be out there for perhaps a week. I don't know Los Angeles too well. I need someone who does know it—and I don't mean just the freeway system."

"What d'you want him to do for you?"

"Drive, run a few errands, answer any questions I might have or, if he can't answer them, know where I should go to ask them."

"How much you willing to spend?"

"Thirty bucks a day. If we use his car, fifty."

Mickey Cupini got interested. We were talking about how much someone should be paid and naturally it wasn't enough. It never would be for Cupini. He leaned forward and rested his elbows on the table. He was wearing a nice dark grey suit that retailed for not much more than three hundred dollars. I liked his pale grey shirt and the dark grey-and-maroon striped tie that flounced a little before it dived down behind his vest. He smoothed the brown hair that just barely covered his ears and his collar and let me look at the gleam in his brown eyes. I decided that it was his negotiation gleam and I wondered how the mayor felt about it when it came time to talk new contract.

Cupini sighed and frowned and the frown caused two deep vertical lines to run down his forehead until they almost touched the start of his long, thin nose. His wide mouth went down at the corners. He wagged his stubborn chin a couple of times. Then he made a little deprecatory motion with his right hand. I looked to see whether he was still wearing his Sigma Chi ring. He was.

"If you just wanted somebody to drive for you, Phil, well, hell, thirty bucks a day wouldn't be bad. I mean it wouldn't be good, but it wouldn't be bad. But, Christ, you don't want just a driver. You want somebody *smart*, with connections, maybe even with a Ph.D., and you think you can get somebody like that for a lousy thirty bucks?"

"A recession is abroad in the land, Mickey. Perhaps

117

even a depression. I'm not on an expense account. It's my own money and it's been a bad year. Thirty-five."

"Forty-five, at least."

I shook my head. "Forty and if we use his car fifty-five, and I pay for the gas."

The gleam in Cupini's eye turned into a glint. We had just struck a bargain. "I know just the guy."

"Who?"

"My wife's brother-in-law's cousin. He's a nice kid. Twenty-two, twenty-three, maybe. And smart."

"What's his name?"

"Giovanni Guerriero, but you can call him Johnny. Everybody else does."

"What does Johnny do when he's not working for me?"

"Sometimes he goes to school. So far he's been to UCLA, Georgetown in Washington, Dartmouth, and the University of Texas."

"And when he's not going to school?"

"He's done a little organizing for us out on the Coast. Then for a while he worked for a cousin of mine in Vegas. You know, muscle work, but the kid didn't like it and quit. He's got a few weird ideas. Maybe that's because he's hooked."

"On what?"

"Politics," Cupini said. "The kid's a political junkie."

"Okay," I said. "He's hired. How do I get in touch with him?"

Cupini looked at his watch. "What's your flight number?"

I told him.

"United?"

"Yes."

"Okay, when we get through lunch, I'll go back to the office and call the kid and have him meet you at the airport. Forty bucks a day or fifty-five if you use his car. Right?"

"Right."

"You just got yourself one hell of a good kid."

"And you're sure he knows L.A.?"

"He should," Mickey Cupini said, "he was born on the Hollywood freeway."

My flight left Kennedy at 9:15 that night. We flew for a little over six hours and with the time change we landed at Los Angeles International at 12:35. The flight had been what is often described as uneventful, which means dull.

At Los Angeles airport I went directly from the plane into a reception area. I was among the last of the passengers off and when I came out into the reception area I spotted Giovanni Guerriero whom I was going to call Johnny.

He was about average height for the young in California, which meant that he was at least six feet tall. It may be because of the sunshine and the vitamins and Dr. Spock, but the average height of both males and females in California during the last twenty years must have risen by at least three inches. He was wearing blue jeans, a short-sleeved shirt, loafers, and a slightly worried expression. I knew he was Johnny Guerriero because of the neatly printed sign that he displayed, which read, "Mr. St. Ives, This Way Please." I felt that we were off to a good start. Maybe he was as smart as Mickey Cupini said he was.

I went up to him and said, "I'm Philip St. Ives."

He gave me a big white grin and put out his hand. "Hi, Phil. I'm Johnny Guerriero." That was nice. I was Phil and he was Johnny and we would probably become great chums. In New York there were people who had known me rather well for fifteen years but who still called me Mr. St. Ives. But they were mostly old fogeys in their late thirties or early forties.

Johnny Guerriero led the way. We walked for a while and then we got on a moving sidewalk and rode a bit, perhaps a block or so, and then we walked some more and finally we got to where they let you pick up your luggage, providing that they haven't lost it.

While we were waiting for my bag we talked about the weather, which Guerriero said had been mild and warm and when I told him about the snow that had hit most of the East Coast last week he said that he hadn't had much to do with snow since he left Dartmouth a couple of years ago.

"You're not going to school now?" I said.

"No, I don't think I'll go back until after the election."

"What election?"

"The presidential one."

"That's this year."

"Yeah, I know. I'm trying to decide who to hook up with."

"Mickey mentioned that you were interested in politics."

Guerriero grinned. "Did he say that I was a political junkie? He usually does."

"I think he might have said something like that."

"I started eight years ago when I was fifteen. I was up in New Hampshire with Gene."

"McCarthy?"

"Yeah."

"It seems longer ago than that."

"Yeah, it does, doesn't it? Then I was in Chicago for the convention and I damned near got killed there. Then I went down to Mississippi for Humphrey and that was one fuckin' lost cause. After that I came back out here and started at UCLA, but by 1970 I was organizing full time for the peace movement and I was at Kent State when all the crap happened. After that I spent a year at Georgetown and worked in a congressman's office part time and then I hooked up with McGovern and went back up to New Hampshire and then out to Minnesota and when he got clobbered, I tried Dartmouth for a while, but I didn't like the weather so I quit and transferred to Texas down in Austin and worked a congressional campaign down there in '74 and then went to Vegas for a while."

"What'd you do in Vegas?"

"Whatever they thought was necessary. I didn't happen to agree with their idea of necessity, so I quit. But I did get a good look at the slimier side of life, if you're interested in that kind of thing. From what Mickey tells me, that's sort of the side of the street you work."

"Sort of," I said.

"You interested in politics?"

"I vote," I said. "But that's about all—unless you count a growing feeling of despair."

He nodded understandingly. "A lot of guys your age feel that way."

121

When my bag arrived I let him carry it so that I could save my strength. At my age, I might need it. We crossed over to a parking lot and stopped in front of a green Ford van.

"Is this it?' I said.

"Uh-huh." He opened the rear door and put the bag in. "I've sort of fixed it up inside," he said.

I looked. There was a deep green shag rug on the floor. A raised section supported a thick slab of foam rubber that was long enough and wide enough to serve as either a bed or a couch. A yellow throw rug covered most of the foam rubber. Opposite the bed was a small butane stove that rested on a two-shelf wooden stand that was filled with canned goods, a skillet, a pot, some plates and glasses, and a miscellaneous collection of kitchen utensils. A portable cooler rested on the floor next to the shelves and the stove. On some hooks that came off the wall were three or four hangers that held a sports coat, a couple of pairs of slacks, and a few shirts. I noticed that there was more storage space in a couple of deep drawers that were cleverly fitted into the platform that held the bed.

"You use it to go camping in?" I said.

Guerriero shrugged as he closed the door. "Sometimes," he said. "Sometimes when I'm broke I live in it. They're handy for a lot of things." He grinned again. "I guess that's why they sometimes call them fuck trucks."

I felt even older as I went around the van and got into the passenger's seat. Guerriero slid behind the wheel, started the engine, and backed out.

"I need some place to stay," I said.

122

"You want a hotel or a motel?"

I thought about it. "A motel, I think."

"There's a small one on La Brea that's pretty good," he said.

"Okay."

Past the airport, Guerriero got on to the San Diego freeway going north and then switched to the Santa Monica freeway and we went east for a while. He drove the way that a lot of Californians drive, with smooth, easy motions and careful attention to the rear-view mirror.

On La Brea we went north for almost a mile and then turned into what was called the Riverside motel although I had seen no evidence of a river anywhere. It was a typical cinder-block affair, painted blue and run by a tired looking man in his fifties whose only question was whether I'd be staying more than one night. When I said that I would, he seemed mildly pleased. At least he smiled a little.

Guerriero carried my bag into the motel room and helped me inspect the bath and the bed. There was one of each and everything looked fairly clean and fairly new and about as cozy as a hospital room.

"Is it okay?" he said.

"It's fine."

"What time do you want me to come by tomorrow?"

"Make it about nine-thirty."

"Where do you think we might go?"

"I'm not sure yet," I said. "Why?"

"No reason. Just curious."

"I'll know by nine-thirty."

"Okay," he said and started for the door. He paused

and said, "Well, have a good night," and then he was gone.

I unpacked my bag and then fixed a drink. I drank it sitting there in a chair that was covered in lime green plastic. There must be far lonelier spots than a cheap motel room in a strange city after midnight, but just then I couldn't think of any.

————————— TWELVE

It was warm the next morning, warm for me anyhow, about 60 degrees and cloudy. I had a mediocre breakfast in a coffee shop that I found across the street. When I came back to the motel I called Max Spivey. He wanted to know where I was staying and where I planned to start.

"I thought I'd talk to Maude Goodwater first," I said.

Spivey was silent for a moment. "I suppose that would be all right."

"Why wouldn't it?"

"She's still pretty upset because of Jack Marsh."

"I have to start somewhere."

"She's had to talk to a lot of people in the last few days. We've talked to her. The cops have talked to her. I don't think she really wants to talk to anybody else."

"I'll try to be both polite and brief."

There was another silence that lasted a few seconds

before Spivey said, "Okay. I'll give you her address and phone number." He read off the phone number and I wrote it down. The address was on Malibu Road. "You know where that is?" he said.

"No, but I'll find it."

After Spivey hung up, I looked at my watch. It was 9:15. I wondered if Maude Goodwater would be up yet and decided to find out. She answered the phone on its third ring. She had a low, quiet voice over the telephone. I told her who I was and why I wanted to see her.

"Were you there?" she said.

"Where?"

"In Washington when Jack was killed?"

"Yes. I was there."

There was a silence. I seemed to be running into them that morning. Then she said, "Will you tell me about it?"

"If you'd like me to," I said.

"Yes, I think I would. Where are you staying?"

"At a motel on La Brea."

"Why don't we make it eleven o'clock?"

I told her that eleven would be fine, listened to her directions, and then hung up. After that I sat in the lime green plastic chair and read the *Los Angeles Times* for a while. There was an interesting article about some coyotes that had found their way into Beverly Hills and were causing all sorts of fuss.

When the knock sounded at the door I looked at my watch. It was 9:30. I opened the door and it was Guerriero, wearing a blue shirt, white duck slacks, and loafers. He was also carrying a white paper bag.

"I brought some coffee in case you hadn't had any," he said.

126

"I can use some more," I said. "Come in."

He came in and took two coffee containers out of the paper sack. "How do you take yours?" he said.

"Just sugar."

He ripped open a small packet of sugar, dumped its contents into one of the coffees, stirred it, and handed it to me.

"Thanks," I said. "How far is it to Malibu?"

"This time of day, about thirty or thirty-five minutes. Maybe less."

"We can make it by eleven?"

He nodded. "No problem. We can even take the scenic route. It's slower, but if you don't have to be there until eleven, we've got plenty of time."

"What's the scenic route?"

"Sunset Boulevard all the way to the beach. Or we can take the Santa Monica freeway. Another way is to take Wilshire out to San Vicente. That's pretty quick, too, if you don't like freeways."

"Let's try Sunset," I said.

Sunset Boulevard hadn't changed much since I had last seen it a few years back. It looked a little more seedy perhaps, and the colors might have turned a bit gaudier. You could still get a massage, if you wanted to, or look at some all-nude girls, or have your fortune told, or buy a secondhand Rolls, or even get something to eat and a place to sleep. At the end of the Strip was something new, two tall black glass buildings that had a gloomy, brooding look about them that made me think of twin sentinels who had been posted there to make sure that the gamier backwash of the Strip didn't slop over into the residential section of Beverly Hills.

It was spring in Beverly Hills and in Bel Air and

127

in Brentwood and I decided that, all things considered, it must cost at least five dollars just to grow a daisy there. As we drove past I admired some of the architectural efforts, which would have looked more at home in Virginia or Cape Cod or maybe somewhere south of Paris. But each of them was home to somebody and, as always, I wondered what it was that the people who lived in them sold or produced or provided and whether they felt just a bit uneasy about it all.

Sunset twisted and curved and dipped and rose and dipped again on its way down to the sea. Guerriero kept the van at a steady forty-five, even on the trickier curves, and we slid around them nicely.

As we went past the east gates to Bel Air he jerked a thumb at them. "If we ever have a fuckin' revolution in this country, that's where it's going to start," he said.

"You think so?"

"Yeah. UCLA's right next door, you know, so all you have to do is get the crazies there all fired up. Then the blacks and the Chicanos will come sweeping in from east L.A. and they'll just burn the goddamned place down."

"When do you think it'll happen? The revolution, I mean."

Guerriero shrugged. "Not soon. Things aren't bad enough yet. They're going to have to get real bad, like in the thirties, or worse."

"Where're you going to be when it comes," I said, "on the barricades?"

He gave me a hard, crooked grin. "Out of town," he said.

The Pacific Ocean was grey that day, not blue, and the long heavy swells rolled in and pounded themselves flat on the beach. Some seagulls were out investigating the possibilities for lunch while a number of self-important sandpipers trotted briskly up and down at the edge of the surf, making sure not to get their feet wet. A solitary stroller, his head bent, worked his way down the beach, stopping now and then to kick at something maybe strange and wonderful that lay half buried in the sand.

We rolled along the Pacific Coast Highway with the ocean on our left and some mud cliffs on our right, which gave way to hills that weren't quite mountains. For a while, on the ocean side, there would be a row of some boxy-looking beach houses, a restaurant or two, some shops, and then a stretch of beach bordered by a parking lot. On our right were more shops and houses and fast-food places and delicatessens and then there would be what looked like an almost carefully marked-off stretch of hill and heather, or whatever it is that grows there by the sea, as though somebody had decided that right here we will give them a taste of greenery and then get back to the commercial junk.

It went on like that for seven or eight miles until we came to a small shopping center with a big Market Basket chain food store sign. We stopped at a light at Webb Way, turned left, and right again onto a narrow blacktop road that hugged the beach and was almost completely lined with houses.

"This is it," Guerriero said. "Malibu Road. A lot of them live along here."

"Who?"

"Picture people."

Although there were a couple of architectural adventures among them, most of the houses were of conventional-enough design. A few of them were even small enough to be called cottages, and nearly all of them were built out on pilings that had been driven deep into the sand.

"The Colony's back that way," Guerriero said. "They keep a guard on the gate to discourage the riff-raff. Along here it's not quite so fancy. You can probably buy one of these places for maybe a hundred and fifty or two hundred thousand."

The house numbers along Malibu Road ran high, up into the 24,000's, and the number we were looking for was attached in metal letters to a high brown cinder-block wall that ran for fifty or sixty feet before it ended at a two-car garage. Behind and above the wall I caught a glimpse of a white-graveled, sloping shed roof and some shake shingles, but it was only a glimpse because the high wall did just what it was intended to, which was insure complete privacy.

Guerriero parked the van along the wall in front of a No Parking sign.

"I'll wait for you," he said.

"I shouldn't be long."

I got out of the van and moved down to the wooden gate in the wall. It was open and I went through it. Behind the gate was a patio bordered by all kinds of succulent shrubs and bushes and small twisted trees that seemed to thrive in the sea air. Nearly all of them looked ripe and juicy and just on the verge of bursting into bloom, although I wasn't sure that any of them ever did.

The patio grounds were covered with irregular pieces of slate that had been cleverly fitted together, like a jigsaw puzzle. Growing in the inch-wide cracks between the pieces of slate was green grass, cropped short and carefully tended. Here and there were a couple of lounges for sunning, a round metal table with a glass top, some metal chairs, and a metal barbecue affair with an electric motor to drive the grill.

I crossed the patio and went down three steps and rang an ivory-colored button. The door opened almost immediately and I got my first look at Maude Goodwater.

I must have had a preconceived notion of what she would look like—probably something blond and brittle and tall with too much green eye shadow. But she wasn't very tall, not over five-five, and her hair wasn't blond, but rather a thick, glossy black that hung straight down until it curved up and under itself just at the base of a slender neck.

Her eyes were green, really green like dark wet jade, and her high cheekbones made them seem to slant a little bit, although they probably didn't. She had a nice enough nose and a full wide mouth and perhaps not quite enough chin, although there were many who would probably argue that it was just right.

Altogether it was a striking face, the kind that you would turn to look at because it just escaped being pretty and went into something that was richer than pretty and therefore more memorable. It could even have been beauty, although I'm still not sure.

She wore a sleeveless blue blouse and white pants and white sandals and nothing else, not even makeup, not that she would ever need it with that smooth skin that seemed to glow with its light tan.

She looked at me and tilted her head slightly to one side, as though she were looking at a curious picture that she couldn't quite decide about, and said, "Hello, Mr. St. Ives, I'm Maude Goodwater."

Then she held out her hand and gave mine a firm shake and stood back so that I could go through the door. As I went past her I looked carefully at her green eyes, but they didn't seem to have done much crying recently.

I stood there in a small foyer with its white stucco walls and its cool grey tiles and waited for her to indicate which way we should go. She made a small gesture and I followed her into a large room that somebody had cleverly decorated with the Pacific Ocean.

The glass did it, of course. It ran from floor to ceiling on two sides and it seemed to bring the sea almost into the living room. There was a redwood deck that served to cut off the view of the beach so that, on first glance, the house seemed to be perched out over the ocean.

The sea made it hard to notice the rest of the furniture, but I remembered some easy chairs in muted colors, a couch, a fireplace, some paintings and a few rugs here and there. But it was the ocean that demanded your attention and the only thing in the room that really competed with it was Maude Goodwater.

She indicated that I could try the couch, if I liked, so I sat down. She chose one of the easy chairs.

"It's a remarkable view," I said.

She nodded. "You never get tired of it. I've been trying to save the house, but I'm afraid that's going to be impossible. I'm putting it up for sale. This house, Mr. St. Ives, is all that's left of a rather large fortune accumulated by a man who didn't understand much about money."

"Your father?"

"Yes."

"There's also the book, the Pliny book."

"Yes, I was counting on its sale. There'll be the insurance money now, of course, but most of that will go for back taxes and debts."

"Do you mind if I smoke?"

"Not at all."

I lit a cigarette. That gave me time to think about where I should start. I decided that the beginning would be as good a place as any. It usually is. "I was wondering how you went about finding a buyer for the book?"

"I'm afraid I turned that over to Jack," she said. There was a silence as she looked away from me and out at the ocean. She was still looking at the ocean when she said, "Since Jack was killed I've been trying to sort out my feelings. It hasn't been easy."

"I can imagine."

"I was very fond of Jack." She looked at me. "That's not really true. I loved him. As you probably know, we were living together."

I nodded since there was really nothing to say.

"When he was killed and I found out what he had done, I didn't stop loving him. I was hurt at first, I suppose, and bitter and deeply disappointed, but I went right on loving him and missing him and damning him for what he had done. I'm just now getting accustomed to thinking of him as dead. I still miss him very much. After a while, maybe I'll learn to hate him, but I don't think so because it would be such a waste of time. So to help me get over it, I mean all of it, it might be best if you told me how he got killed. It might help me realize—well, the finality of it all."

She turned her head to look at the ocean while I told her. When I described how Fastnaught had come out of the snow to shoot Jack Marsh a tremor ran through her body but nothing changed in her face. She turned to look at me.

"So it wasn't a trick? I mean you were really trying to buy the book back?"

"Yes."

She smiled, but there was more regret in it than anything else. "Although I knew it wasn't possible, I was hoping that you would turn out to be something entirely different."

"Such as?"

"Oh, I don't know. Maybe somebody who had a cigar stub in his mouth and looked slightly sinister and conspiratorial. Somebody I could blame for Jack's death and who would confess that it was all a horrible mistake and that Jack was innocent."

I shook my head. "He wasn't."

"No, I know that. I haven't accepted it yet, but I know it."

"I wonder if we could get back to how you, or Marsh, I suppose, went about finding a buyer for the book?"

Maude Goodwater rose and moved over to the glass and looked out at the sea. "Hindsight is very useful, isn't it?"

"Useful and painful," I said.

"I had gone over my financial situation with my attorney. I won't bother you with the mess I'm in, but it's bad. Very bad. So it was decided that I should sell this place and the book. By doing so I could pay off the debts and the taxes and have something left over. Not too much, but enough to last a year or so. I discussed it with Jack, of course, and he offered to arrange for the sale of the book. He said he had certain contacts that he could use to secure the highest possible price. I believed him, of course. Why shouldn't I?"

"No reason."

She turned from the glass and the sea and came back to the chair and sat down. "Jack brought a man out to see me, a most curious little man. I don't mean to use 'little' in the pejorative sense, but the man was really quite small."

"Did he have a name?" I said.

"Ambrose. Felix Ambrose. We discussed the book and Ambrose seemed quite knowledgeable. He used all sorts of rather esoteric jargon that sounded most impressive—to me, at least. He said that he had a buyer for the book who would pay seven hundred and fifty thousand dollars, but who insisted on anonymity."

"How much would Ambrose get?"

"He asked for two percent as his finder's fee."

"Fifteen thousand dollars?"

"Yes."

"Did he ask for any in advance?"

"No. He didn't."

"Did he say why the buyer insisted on remaining anonymous?"

"He said that the buyer was very rich and very eccentric and hated publicity of any kind."

"But was just crazy about rare old books."

"Yes, I suppose that's the impression I got. I must be awfully naive. There probably never was a buyer, was there?"

"I don't know," I said. "But I'm beginning to doubt

135

if there was one who was willing to pay three-quarters of a million."

"It's so ridiculous, isn't it? I've told all this to the police and to some insurance company investigators that Max Spivey asked me to see, and every time I tell it I have the feeling that I'm not talking about myself. I seem to be talking about some innocent little old lady who's just been fleeced out of her life savings. But that's not me. I always thought of myself as rather—well, I guess worldly. I watched my father die a broken man. I went through a nasty marriage and an even worse divorce. I've had my share of lovers—both men and women, if that matters. I've tried drugs. I even got terribly rebellious once and tried earning my own living for a couple of years and that was a real eye-opener. So I thought I knew what it was all about—out there in the big world where bad things happen. But this—" She shook her head. "This is just absurd."

"You can't blame yourself," I said. "You got taken by someone you seem to have loved and trusted. It wouldn't make it hurt any less for me to tell you how often it happens, so I won't."

She used a forefinger to wipe something away from her left eye. It may have been a tear although I don't think so.

"It does happen to other people, doesn't it?"

"Every day."

"And what do they do about it?"

"Just about what you're doing. They blame themselves mostly. After a while they get angry, really angry, and when the anger's directed at somebody else instead of themselves it seems to help. Not much, but some."

136

She chewed on her lower lip for a while as if thinking about something. "You haven't given me any great advice, have you?"

"No."

"But talking about it helps, doesn't it? Just talking about it."

"Almost always. If I weren't here, you could find a priest or a psychiatrist or just somebody on a park bench. The result is often pretty much the same."

"Would you like a drink?"

"Sure, if you're having one."

"I am," she said and rose and moved over to a small bar that was near the dining table, which was the kind that had a chrome frame and legs and a glass top.

"It's not too early for martinis, is it?"

"Probably."

"Well, we'll have one anyway."

She mixed them in a small pitcher and poured them into a couple of glasses. She carried them over and handed me one. After she took a sip she tried to grin and she almost made it. "Okay," she said, "what else do you want to know about that son of a bitch, Jack Marsh?"

I smiled at her. "A couple of personal things."

"Go ahead."

"What kind of financial shape was he in?"

"Well, we had one of those oh-so-sensible, oh-so-modern arrangements. He lived here and we split expenses. He gave me a check every month for seven hundred and fifty dollars and I paid the bills—food, the mortgage, utilities, things like that. He was sort of a star boarder, I guess."

"Did he spend a lot?"

She nodded. "He blew it—on clothes and that car of his and the track and in Vegas. I guess all I really know is that he was always broke. Or said he was."

"What about his business?"

"He worked hard, I'll say that for him. But we never talked much about it. His cases, I mean. When he moved in here he moved his office from Hollywood out to Santa Monica. The commuting was better."

"Did he have anybody working for him?"

"Just a secretary. Her name's Virginia Neighbors and she's in the book."

"You wouldn't have a key to his office, would you?"

Maude Goodwater looked at me over the rim of her glass. "You know, I thought there was something familiar about you."

"What?"

"You ask questions the same way he used to. Jack, I mean. There's that same low-key inflection. Both of you would ask the time of day the same way you'd say, 'And after you got through stabbing him with the butcher knife, Mrs. Smith, what did you do then?' "

"It's sort of a trick," I said.

"Did you used to be a detective?"

"No. I was a reporter once."

"Same thing."

"Detectives don't think so, although some reporters do. What about the key?"

She went over and picked up her purse from where it was lying in a leather chair. She took out a ring and removed one key. She looked at it and then came over and handed it to me. "I wonder if that's smart?" she said.

"I'm trying to find out what happened. Whether it's smart or not depends on whether you really want to know."

"No matter what?"

"No matter what."

"Uh-huh," she said. "I think I do. At first, all I wanted to do was forget it, but now I think I want to find out what he was really like. I'm still not sure. I've got the feeling that I've been living with some stranger."

"When I find out something, I'll let you know."

She looked around the room. "You like it out here?"

"Very much."

"Maybe when you find out something, you could come to dinner. I'm a pretty good cook. What I'm really saying is that I'm probably not through wanting to talk about it and I just don't want to go down to a park to find a friendly ear. Maybe . . . maybe we could even get to be friends. I've never been that with a man. You know, just friends."

"We could try," I said.

"I've talked a lot, haven't I?"

"Not really."

"Nothing else you'd like to know?"

"Is there something else you remember about the little man, Felix Ambrose?"

She wrinkled her forehead, trying to remember. "He was about five feet tall and he dressed rather oddly. I mean for out here. He wore one of those old-fashioned salt and pepper suits with a vest and a bow tie and he spoke well, but as if he had somehow trained himself to do it. You know what I mean?"

I nodded and closed my eyes for a moment because something was happening to my memory. Something was poking at it, trying to tear through. Closing my eyes didn't help so I opened them and said, "Anything else?"

She thought for a moment. "Jack called him Doc a couple of times. Not Doctor, but Doc. I didn't think anything of it then, but I do now."

The sharp stick that had been poking at my memory tore through. I sighed. "He carried a cane, didn't he? A silver-headed cane."

The surprise in her face was real. "Why, yes, he did. I'd almost forgotten. You know him, don't you?"

"I did a long time ago, but his name isn't Felix Ambrose, it's really Harry Amber, although sometimes he's called Doc Amber because after he got through being a jockey he doped racehorses, and after he got out of jail for doing that, he turned himself into a pretty successful con man down in Florida—Miami mostly, but sometimes Palm Beach."

"Then it was a fake from the beginning, wasn't it? This man Ambrose or Amber couldn't possibly have had a buyer for the book."

"Not necessarily," I said. "Doc Amber knows a lot of people. When you told the police about him, did they seem to know who he was?"

"No, they just wanted to know whether I knew how to get in touch with him or where he lived."

"What'd you tell them?"

"I told them to try the phone book."

----------------- **THIRTEEN**

Maude Goodwater and I talked for a little more than an hour. Mostly I listened while she told me how it had been, living with Jack Marsh, and how they had sometimes gone up to San Francisco on weekends, or down to Ensenada, or sometimes they had just stayed home and played records or walked along the beach.

She made it sound so idyllic that I asked her when Jack Marsh had found time to tend to his gambling. She told me that he was a plunger and that when he gambled he usually did it by himself, sometimes spending as much as a week or ten days in Las Vegas. He also liked the tracks. When he lost, which he did often, she said that he hadn't been very pleasant to be around.

It was shortly after noon when I left her and went out to the Ford van. Guerriero was slumped down in the front seat behind the wheel reading a paperback edition of Camus' *Lyrical and Critical Essays*.

"You should read that when you're about forty," I told him.

"Why?"

"It confirms what you suspected at twenty."

He grinned and put the book up behind the sun visor. "Where to?"

"Santa Monica, but first maybe we should get some lunch. Is there any place you can recommend around here?"

He nodded as he started the engine. "There's a place just down the highway that's not too bad," he said. "Some of the help's kind of pretty anyhow."

The place he suggested turned out to be the Crazy Horse Saloon which had been decorated in a halfway serious attempt to make it resemble something out of the wild west or what nearly everybody, after half a century or so of Hollywood westerns, thought a wild west saloon should look like providing it was air-conditioned. Actually, the hamburgers weren't at all bad although I have found that you seldom go wrong if you order a hamburger in Los Angeles, which is more than can be said for the rest of the nation. Also, the pretty girl who served us didn't at all seem to mind being a waitress and she and Guerriero got to do some friendly flirting.

The sun had burned through the haze and the clouds by the time we got to Santa Monica and the ocean was back to being blue. Some oldsters were walking slowly and carefully beneath the tall palms in the narrow green park along Ocean Avenue. The oldsters looked the way a lot of retired people do—neat and clean and bored stiff.

Guerriero swung left on Santa Monica and we found a place to park without too much trouble in a metered zone near the corner of Second and Santa Monica. There was some traffic, but not too much. A few pedestrians went by, taking their time. It all looked bright and well-swept and about half asleep. I must have shaken my head because Guerriero again gave me his hard, white grin and said, "It's not quite New York, is it?"

"Not quite."

"You ought to see it about midnight."

"What happens then?"

"Well, for excitement you can go out and bay at the moon."

Most of the tenants of the bank building that Jack Marsh had his office in seemed to be either lawyers or dentists. Marsh's office was on the sixth floor and I got into the elevator with a cheerful old party who told me that he was on his way up to have his last tooth pulled. When I told him that was too bad he cackled happily and said, "Hell, son, it's something to do."

After I let myself in with the key that Maude Goodwater had given me I saw that Jack Marsh had spent some money on furnishing his office. There were two rooms to it, the smaller outer office for his secretary, and the larger inner office where he had done his heavy thinking.

The door that led from the corridor into the suite had only Jack Marsh lettered on it and nothing else. Not Discreet Inquiries Undertaken or Private Investigator or even Walk In. There was a terribly modern desk of pale blond wood for his secretary and a typewriter that was protected with a grey IBM cover. On her desk there was nothing but the phone, a small calendar, and a glass vase, just large enough to hold a single white rose. The rose looked fresh. I looked around the rest of the room. There were three comfortable looking chairs upholstered in pale tan or beige that were clustered around a coffee table whose glass top was supported by a base of polished chrome. The carpet was dark brown and thick. On the walls were a couple of prints and in the corner a coatrack.

I moved over to the desk and thumbed through the calendar. It was the kind whose pages turned on two metal hasps. I went back to the first of April and worked my way forward. All the notes were written in short-hand except for a few names that didn't mean anything to me. I wrote the names down on an envelope anyway, feeling a little foolish. After that I tried the desk drawers, but they were locked.

Jack Marsh had done himself well in his own office. There was a nice big polished rosewood desk and behind it a high-backed chair that looked as if it were covered in real leather instead of Naugahyde and in front of the desk were some comfortable looking chairs expensively covered in something that looked like suede but probably wasn't. In one corner were three brown metal file cabinets that I didn't even bother with because they were secured with padlocked metal poles that ran through their drawer handles just like they are at the CIA.

I went around the desk and sat down in the fine big swivel chair and tried the drawers. They weren't locked. I wasn't sure what I expected to find that the police hadn't already found, but I went through the motions anyway. Maybe the police had missed something taped to the bottom of one of the drawers. They hadn't, of course. They never do.

But there was some recent correspondence that Marsh had had with a manufacturer who was being robbed silly by some of his employees. Marsh had cleared that up nicely and the manufacturer had been so grateful that he had given Marsh a bonus.

There was more correspondence with another client concerning Marsh's fees. The client thought they were a little high and Marsh had had to explain how they could have been even higher, if it hadn't been for Marsh's years of experience, diligence, and general acumen, which had enabled him to solve the client's problem (where his wife went on Thursday afternoons) long before Marsh's competition could have come up with the same answer. I felt that Jack Marsh wrote a nice letter.

The only thing that I found tucked away out of sight were some bills with either Past Due or Final Notice stamped on them. They were from men's clothing stores, a sporting goods shop, and a mechanic who specialized in Porsches.

In the center drawer of the desk was a red address book. I went through it. Some of the names and addresses and phone numbers had been entered in what I recognized as the secretary's pretty round hand. I skipped those and concentrated on the ones that apparently had been entered by Marsh. They were written in a blocky kind of penmanship that seemed more concerned with legibility than style. I went through the

145

book twice before I caught it. In the D's at the bottom of the page written lightly in pencil was "Doc" and a phone number.

I took the envelope that I had used earlier and wrote the number down. I had just finished when I heard the door to the outer office open and close. I put the red address book back in the top drawer and stood up. Someone coughed once in the outer office. I thought it sounded like a woman's cough, but I wasn't sure because there isn't that much difference between the way that men and women cough.

After the cough it was very quiet again and I thought I could hear my own breathing. I listened hard and heard the sound of a paper match being struck. It popped a little, the way they sometimes do.

She came through the door then, smoking a cigarette. She jumped when she saw me and opened her mouth and I wasn't sure whether she was going to scream so I said, "Maude Goodwater gave me a key." I fished the key out of my pocket and held it up so that she could see it.

"This isn't her office," the woman said. "She had no right to do that."

"You must be Virginia Neighbors," I said. "I was going to call you."

She remembered the cigarette that she was holding and brought it up to her lips and inhaled some smoke. She blew it out in a long, thin plume, staring at me.

"Okay," she said. "You know me, but I don't know you."

I looked at her for a moment before saying anything. She had a goggley look about her because of the enormous round purple sunglasses that she was wearing. They seemed to be more darkly tinted at their tops than at their bottoms. I couldn't see her eyes because of them. I could see her hair though. It was blond and parted in the center and it fell down her back. How far, I couldn't tell. She had a full red mouth that lipstick had made even redder and it might have looked kissable to some, but it looked only pouty to me, although that might have been the way that she always looked when she was angry or surprised or even both. Beneath her mouth and to the left was a small brown mole, almost a beauty mark. Her nose, I remember, was pink and shiny.

"My name's St. Ives."

"That still doesn't tell me anything."

"I was there when Jack Marsh got shot," I said and waited to see what that did for her.

Her lower lip trembled, until she caught it between her teeth. I went over to where she was standing, reached up and gently took the dark glasses off. She had round blue eyes whose whites were so red that they looked almost inflamed. I handed her the glasses.

"Go ahead," I said. "You should cry some more if it helps."

She was wearing a pale tan pants suit with a dark brown sweater and I noticed that she had nice breasts. I still notice things like that. I probably always will. The jacket of the pants suit had pockets and she reached into one of them and brought out a pink wad of Kleenex and blew her nose into it.

"I'm not going to cry," she said, putting the dark glasses back on and stuffing the Kleenex back into her pocket. She had managed to hold on to the cigarette

147

through all of this and she took another drag from it, inhaling the smoke deeply.

"Are you a cop?" she said, blowing the smoke out.

"No."

"But you were there when he got shot?"

"Yes."

"Then you must be that guy from New York, the go-between. I heard about you, but I didn't remember your name."

"Who told you about me?"

"The cops. The L.A. cops. They were here yesterday and last week, right after—well, right after it happened. They went through everything. But not until I made sure they had a warrant. Then they asked me a lot of dumb questions."

"Such as?"

"Why should I tell you?"

"No reason. I'm just trying to find out what really happened."

"He got shot. Killed. That's what happened."

"I know. I was there."

"Did he—" She stopped to bite her lip again. "Did it hurt him much? I mean did he suffer?"

"No. It was over in a second."

"Did he—well, did he say anything?"

I decided to give her something to keep. It wouldn't do any harm and perhaps on those long nights to come she could take it out and fondle it and perhaps play "might have been" with it.

"He muttered something—just one word. It sounded something like 'Virgie,' but I wasn't sure what it meant so I never told anyone about it."

148

Her chin trembled and then her nose turned even pinker and her mouth opened and she started to bawl in earnest. She took off the dark glasses so she could dab at her eyes again with the Kleenex. I went over and patted her on the shoulder and said something meaningless like, "Come on now," and, "There, there."

It was over after a minute or so and she put the dark glasses back on. "He called me that most of the time. Virgie, I mean."

That hadn't been hard to guess. I felt that I was getting to know Jack Marsh better and so far I hadn't found much to like. I smiled at her. "You and he must have been very close."

She nodded. "I worked for him for five years."

"I meant close personally."

"I knew him better than anybody," she said. "Even better than her."

"Miss Goodwater?"

"Miss Rich Bitch. I told him he was making a mistake when he moved in with her." She nodded her head the way people do when they've been right and everyone else has been wrong. "I told him. And just look what happened."

I wondered how old she was. With her glasses off and her eyes red and her nose all shiny she looked about ten but she talked like forty. Or maybe fifty. I guessed her to be thirty. Maybe thirty-two.

"But you kept on working for him even after he started living with Maude Goodwater."

"Sure I did. Why shouldn't I?"

I shrugged. I tried to make it an elaborate one. Her lip curled up and for a moment I thought she was going to cry again, but I was wrong. It was a sneer. "We didn't stop fucking just because he moved in with her." That was her best pitch, the high, hard one, and she waited to see how I handled it.

I decided to watch it go by. "There's just a chance," I said, "that somebody set Jack up."

"What do you mean set him up?" she said. "A cop shot him. A Washington cop with a funny name."

"Fastnaught."

"Yeah. That's it. Fastnaught."

"Jack wasn't working this thing alone, you know," I said, feeling odd about calling him Jack. "He had teamed up with somebody. Maybe this somebody tipped Fastnaught off. Let's face it. Whoever was in it with Jack made off with a quarter of a million dollars plus the old book. All Jack got was dead."

I didn't know how much the Los Angeles police had told her, but I doubted that they had described how Fastnaught had tailed me out to Haines Point in the snow. It was one of those details that they probably wouldn't have bothered to tell her. Jack Marsh had been shot and killed by a Washington cop. That was the big news and it should have been enough.

Her face was working itself up into another crying spell. I took out my handkerchief and handed it to her. She blew her nose with it and stuffed it into her pocket, not thinking about what she was doing. I didn't ask for it back.

"I don't know who was in it with him," she said dully. "I keep hoping that they'll find out that somebody made him do it. Held a gun to his head, you know, and made him do it. But I don't guess there's much chance of that, is there?"

"Not much."

She produced another cigarette from her jacket pocket and held it up. It took a second before I realized that she was waiting for me to light it. I found my matches and lit it and then looked around for an ashtray. I found one on the desk where she had ground out the one that she was smoking before. I put the match in it. When I turned back she was chewing on her lower lip as if trying to decide how much she could tell me. I waited for her to make up her mind.

"I knew something funny was going on," she said.

"You did, huh? How?"

"Because he didn't talk about it. He always talked about them with me. His cases, I mean. Even after he moved out there to Malibu he talked them over with me because I understood what it was that he did. He was like any man. He liked to be oohed and ahed over and told how smart he was. She couldn't do that because she didn't understand what he did for a living and so he didn't talk about it with her. I sometimes wondered what they did talk about. Maybe how beautiful the sunset was and crap like that. Lovey-dovey stuff."

"He didn't tell you anything about it at all?"

"He told me he had to go to Washington and pick something up and bring it back. He didn't say what."

"Did he say who? I mean who was going to pay him?"

"Sure. Max Spivey at Pacifica was going to pay him.

But there wasn't any big deal about it. He did a lot of work for Max. The only funny thing was he wouldn't tell me what he was going to pick up in Washington."

"Did you ask?"

"Sure I asked. That's when it got funny. When he wouldn't tell me."

"In that week before he went to Washington," I said. "Did he see Doc Amber?"

"Who?"

"Doc Amber. A little guy about five feet tall. He uses a lot of big words and wears what used to be called snappy clothes."

She shook her head slowly. "He didn't know anybody like that. I'd remember it if he knew anybody like that."

"Well, thanks for talking to me," I said. "I know it must be difficult for you."

She looked around the room and shook her head. "I don't even know why I come down here. Nobody's paying me. I don't know if anybody ever will. I just check the mail and write a few letters. I talked to his lawyer about it but he's not even sure about what's going to happen. The rent's paid to the end of the month. I guess I'll just keep on coming down until then and after that I won't come any more."

"It's nice of you to do it."

She looked at me, or at least those big purple glasses did. "You weren't kidding me about that, were you? You know about him saying 'Virgie' and all. You couldn't make something like that up, could you?"

"No." I said. "I couldn't make something like that up. Nobody could."

FOURTEEN

Downstairs in the lobby I found a pay phone and called the number that I had copied from Jack Marsh's address book. It rang twice and then somebody, a man, answered and said, "Yeah?"

"Doc Amber, please," I said, trying to be brisk and businesslike.

"He ain't here."

"When do you think he might be in?"

"How the hell should I know? I ain't his secretary. Who's this?"

"Just a friend."

"Well, lemme tell you something, just a friend, he ain't here and I don't know when he's gonna be here, if he is."

"Maybe I could drop by and see him."

"Maybe you could."

"What's the best time?"

"Like I said, how the hell should I know?"

"Maybe I could come by and wait for him."

"I don't give a shit what you do."

"I'm not sure that I've got that address down right."

There was a silence. Then the man said, "You say you're just a friend of Doc's, huh?"

"That's right."

"But you ain't got this address?"

"I'm not sure that I've got it right."

"Fuck off, Jack," the man said and hung up.

I went back out to the van and climbed in. Guerriero started the engine. "Where to?" he said.

I handed him the envelope on which I'd written the number that I'd just called. "We've got a problem," I said. "That number. I'd like to get an address to go with it."

Guerriero tucked the envelope into a pocket. "No problem," he said. "Not if you're willing to spend twenty bucks."

"I'm willing."

It was a thirty-minute ride. We took the Santa Monica freeway into Los Angeles and got off at La Brea. We went north on La Brea and then turned east down Melrose until we came to a row of small shops on the right-hand side of the street. The shops sold a variety of things including health foods and antiques and paintings. The one we stopped in front of was called the Fat Attic and most of the stuff in its window seemed to be old clothes and odds and ends from the thirties and the forties and even the twenties.

In the center of the row of shops was a passageway that led back toward the rear. With Guerriero leading we went down the passageway until we came to a door. Guerriero knocked and the door was opened after a moment by a girl with long red hair and a freckled face. She couldn't have been much more than nineteen.

"Is he in?" Guerriero said.

The girl nodded. "He's always in. Who's he?" she said, looking at me.

"A customer," Guerriero said.

The girl looked at me some more and then stepped back, opening the door. Guerriero and I went into a room that held a couch, a couple of chairs, a round table with a Formica top, and a big old Philco radio, the floor console kind whose dial was tipped back at an angle. I remembered vaguely that when they were advertising those tipped-back dials in the forties the selling pitch had been, "No Stoop, No Squat, No Squint." The radio was on and playing some kind of background music that was as memorable as wallpaper.

The girl went to a door and opened it. "It's Guerriero," she called.

A young man came through the doorway, lightly brushing its sides with his fingertips. He wasn't quite as young as the girl, perhaps a year or two older, and his skin was white and pasty as though he never got out into the sun. He turned his head in our direction, but he didn't really look at us. He couldn't. He was blind.

"How are you?" he said.

"Not bad," Guerriero said. "What about you?"

The blind man shrugged. "What do you need?"

"An address to fit a number," Guerriero said.

The man nodded. "What's the number?"

Guerriero read it off from the envelope that I'd written it on. The blind man nodded again. "Twenty bucks," he said.

I took out my wallet and removed a twenty-dollar

bill. It didn't make much noise, hardly any, in fact, but the blind man heard it. "Give it to her," he said.

I handed the bill to the girl and the blind man must have heard that, too, because he said, "Sorry, but I don't give receipts."

"That's all right," I said. It was the first time that I had said anything.

The blind man cocked his head to one side. "About thirty-five," he said. "Maybe forty. Maybe six feet tall, but maybe a little less. You lived back east, but originally you came from the Midwest, Cleveland?"

"That's close," I said. "Columbus."

He nodded and smiled a little, but not very much. "The 'a' in your 'all' was pure Ohio, but you sort of spit your 't's' the way they do back in New York and Jersey."

"I'll have to watch it," I said.

He shrugged. "It's just a hobby. I'll be back in a minute." He turned and went through the open door, closing it behind him.

The redheaded girl made a vague gesture. "Sit down someplace, if you want to. He won't be long. All he has to do is call the phone company."

"I didn't know they were so cooperative," I said.

She looked at me. "Are you kidding?"

Guerriero sat down at the Formica table. "He's a master phone freak," he said. "He's been doing it since he was six. He knows all the phone company jargon so when he calls in on a special number he's got they think it's just some other employee asking for legitimate information. Most of the time he just sells unlisted phone numbers. Movie stars. You want to talk to your favorite movie star?"

"Not especially," I said.

"He'll sell you the number for ten bucks."

"We got a new thing going," the girl said.

"What?" Guerriero said.

"He's figured out a way to tap into any phone number. You know when you call in and ask the operator to verify if a number's really busy or just off the hook?"

"Yeah."

"Well, when she checks it he's figured out a way to stay plugged into it. Then he hooks up a tape recorder and when anybody talks on the number the tape recorder goes to work. He can do that on any number so if you wanta hear what kinda phone calls your favorite movie star makes in a twenty-four hour period, we'll sell it to you for a hundred bucks."

Guerriero shook his head. "That's going to get you in trouble. That really will."

The girl moved her shoulders in an elaborate shrug. "We need the bread."

The blind kid opened the door and came back into the room a few moments later. He turned his head to one side and then to the other as if trying to sense whether any of us had moved. He turned so that he was facing Guerriero, or almost. He was just a shade off.

"It's a bar over on Pico," he said. "The Happy Pelican. I wrote the address down on this." He took two steps and held out a slip of paper to Guerriero and the movement wasn't more than an inch or two off from the way that a person with sight would have done it.

Guerriero took the paper and put it in his pocket. "She told us about your new deal," he said. "The taped phone calls."

The blind young man smiled, but again it was a

very small smile. "It's not as bad as it sounds," he said. "If there's anything on them would embarrass anybody, I wipe it. Most of the time it's just dumb talk between them and their agents."

"It's going to get you in trouble," Guerriero said. "Somebody's going to talk and they'll fuck you over good."

"I could always weave baskets, couldn't I?" the blind kid said.

"Well, it's your ass," Guerriero said as he rose from the table and turned toward the door.

The blind kid turned with him. "See you around," he said.

The Happy Pelican looked like a bar that sold a lot of draft beer and not too much Scotch. It was housed in a narrow building that had a bricked-up front and a heavy slab wooden door. For decoration somebody had come up with a large cartoon figure of a pelican fashioned out of blue neon. The pelican's smile winked on and off. For some reason they had also stuck a monocle in his left eye. I didn't think the pelican looked very happy. In fact, I thought he looked a little morose and embarrassed about the whole idea.

Guerriero parked the van around the corner on a side street.

"You want a beer?" I said.

"Do you really want to buy me a beer or do you just want company in there in case the guy you're looking for doesn't want to be found and things get maybe a bit impolite?"

"He's only five feet tall," I said. "He couldn't hurt a sick fly."

"Maybe he's got friends."

"Maybe," I said.

"Well, what the hell," Guerriero said. "I was thirsty anyhow."

It was already twilight in the Happy Pelican. They probably liked it that way even in the morning when the early drinkers arrived. Guerriero and I slid onto a couple of stools at the end of the bar and looked around.

Opposite the bar was a row of booths that ran back to a couple of doors labeled His and Hers. Centered between the doors was a jukebox that was mercifully silent. Along the bar were scattered six or seven serious drinkers, most of whom seemed to be reading the labels on the bottles. Those who weren't reading the labels were gazing out into space with that look that people get when they're recalling past disasters. One of them was moving his lips. Only two of them looked up at us when we came in. The rest didn't bother.

The bartender was at the far end of the bar using a small Tensor lamp to read something in a folded newspaper. It looked like a box score. When he was through reading it he put the newspaper down and moved toward us. He was about forty or forty-five and he wasn't very tall, but he was awfully wide with heavy arms and shoulders and wrists that were as thick as beer bottles. When he reached us he rested for a while, leaning against the bar on his folded arms and looking us over with his ice-colored eyes. After he was through doing that he said, "What'll it be, gents?"

"A couple of beers," I said. "Schlitz."

"A couple of Schlitz," he said and when he spoke this time I was almost sure that it was the same voice

159

that hadn't been overly friendly when I had called earlier to ask about Doc Amber.

The bartender went away to get the beer and when he came back I pushed a twenty-dollar bill across the bar. "I'd still like to get in touch with Doc Amber," I said.

The bartender looked at me carefully and then poured some beer into Guerriero's glass. After that he poured some into mine and we watched the foam mount together. Then he sat my bottle down with a hard bang and I jumped a little. Not much, though.

"You're the party that called earlier," he said.

"Yeah, I had the right address after all."

"Uh-huh."

"What time do you think Doc might be in?"

The bartender folded his big arms and again used them to lean on with. I could smell his breath. He had been drinking bourbon and chasing it with Clorets. He stared at me some more. After he tired of that he unfolded his arms and ran a thick finger down my tie and gave the end of it a little flick.

"Nice tie," he said. "Must have cost you a few bucks."

"A few."

"Nice jacket, too. Real wool tweed, ain't it? None of that synthetic crap."

"That's right," I said. "Real wool tweed."

"I can't see your pants but you probably got a press in them and probably a shine on your shoes. I mean I notice things like that. You know what it spells to me?"

"What?"

"Back east."

"So?"

"So I was talking to Doc Amber earlier today and you know what he told me?"

"What?"

"Doc tells me he don't much wanta talk to certain parties from back east unless he knows who they are. And here's another fact for you. Doc don't much wanta talk to any party, irregardless of where they're from, unless he knows what they want with him. Irregardless, he said."

"I bet he did," I said.

"What d'you mean, friend?"

"Nothing. Just that Doc likes to use big words like that. Irregardless."

"You got any peanuts?" Guerriero said.

The bartender looked at him and gestured with his head. "End of the bar, kid. Your buddy here and me are having a dialogue and I don't wanta interrupt it to go get no peanuts."

"You want some peanuts?" Guerriero said to me. "Or can you chew peanuts and have a dialogue all at the same time?"

"He's a smart-ass kid, ain't he?" the bartender said.

Guerriero smiled at him with his hard, white grin, slid off the stool, and moved toward the rear of the place. The bartender turned his head to check how many packets of peanuts Guerriero got from the end of the bar. Then he turned back to stare at me some more. "Like I was saying," he said, "Doc sorta wants to know who comes in looking for him."

"St. Ives," I said. "Philip St. Ives. Maybe I should write it down on something—maybe on a ten dollar bill."

The bartender used an elbow to shove the twenty

I had placed on the bar toward me. "This'll do," he said. "You got a pen?"

"I've got one." I took out a ball-point pen and wrote my name on the back of the bill in the white space just above the White House. To the right of my name I wrote Riverside motel. I moved the bill back over toward the bartender.

"What d'you want Doc to do?" the bartender said, reading what I had written on the bill.

"Drop by and see me," I said. "I'd like to talk to him."

"What about?"

"A book. A real old book."

"You wanta buy it or sell it?"

"I don't know," I said. "Tell him I just might want to borrow it."

————————————— FIFTEEN

When we got back to the Riverside motel at five I told Guerriero that although I probably wouldn't be needing him that night, I would like a phone number where I could reach him. He wrote one down and gave it to me.

"What time tomorrow?" he said.

"About ten, I guess."

"Are we making any progress?"

"With what?"

"With whatever it is that we're doing."

"I don't know," I said. "I'm not sure."

"But we're going to be doing more of the same tomorrow, whatever it is?"

"Probably."

"You know what's wrong with you?"

"What?" I said.

He grinned. "You talk too much."

After Guerriero drove off I went into the motel

office and checked with the tired looking man to see whether I had had any calls. I hadn't. On the way back to my room I stopped by the ice machine and scooped up a bucketful. Inside my room I got the Scotch out and mixed a drink. Armed with that I moved over to the phone and dialed Myron Greene's home number in Darien, Connecticut. It rang three times before Deborah answered. Deborah was four and we had a nice talk, perhaps four dollars' worth, about her new rabbit, Jimmy, and about Jimmy's funny pink eyes.

Finally Myron Greene came on and I said, "I thought I'd let you know where to reach me."

He told me to hold on while he got something to write it down on. When he came back I gave him the name of the motel and its phone number and the number of the room I was in.

"What if somebody else wants to reach you?" he said.

I thought about it for a moment. "I think you'd better give it to them."

"Anybody at all?"

"That's right. Anybody at all."

"Are you making any progress?"

"I'm asking a lot of questions. I'm not sure whether the answers I'm getting could be called progress though."

"How long do you think it might take?"

"I'm giving it a week. That's all."

"Anything I can do?"

"If you happen to run across a nicely appointed one-bedroom apartment with a view of the river for two hundred bucks a month, you might tell them I'll take it."

"I'll put Joan to work on it. She's good at such stuff." Joan was Myron Greene's secretary. "But I don't think she can find anything like that for two hundred a month."

"I was only kidding, Myron. I'll go a lot higher."

"You know how literal I am when it comes to money."

"Sorry. I forgot. If anything happens out here, I'll let you know."

"All right," he said and after we said good-bye, I hung up. It was still too early to eat so I sipped my drink for a while and finished reading the morning's *Los Angeles Times*. At seven I turned on the television set and looked at the network news and marveled, as I always did, at how much money was spent on bringing so little news to so many.

At seven-thirty I switched off the set and walked down the courtyard toward the motel office. The tired looking man was watching a game show in which the contestants jumped up and down and screamed and hugged the master of ceremonies every few minutes. He seemed to be interested in the show so I didn't say anything until a commercial came on.

"If I get any calls, I'll be back in a few minutes," I said. "I'm just going out to eat. Can you recommend something?"

"Well, you don't wanta try that place across the street."

"I already did. This morning."

"You haven't got a car, have you?"

"No."

"If you don't mind a little walk, there's a rib joint about half a mile down La Brea. You like ribs?"

"Ribs sound good."

"Well, they got pretty good ribs down there. Straight down La Brea on your left. It's called Hank's Rib Joint. You can't miss it, like people always tell me when I ask directions, but, by God, I do. Miss it, I mean."

"I'll try not to."

"You don't mind the walk, huh?"

"No. I don't mind it."

"People in this town don't walk anywhere. I mean, they need a pack of cigarettes and the drugstore's a block away, but you think they walk? Hell, no. They drive. Goddamnedest thing you ever saw."

I thanked the tired looking man for the directions and for sharing his thoughts with me and left. It was pleasantly cool out and there didn't seem to be much smog and I had the broad sidewalk virtually to myself all the way to Hank's Rib Joint where the pork spareribs that I ordered turned out to be every bit as good as the tired looking man had promised.

Back at the motel I sat in the chair that was covered in lime green plastic and smoked cigarettes and waited for something to happen. A little after nine, something did happen. The phone rang. I picked it up and the hard, chipper voice on the other end said, "What the hell you doing in L.A., St. Ives?"

"Looking for you, among other things."

"Yeah, I got your message. What's all this crap about a book?"

"I think we'd better talk about it, Doc."

"Whaddya think we're doing?"

"The phone's not much good for something like this."

"I'm a busy man, St. Ives."

"You know about Jack Marsh, don't you?" I said.

"I know he's dead."

"The cops know that, too. I don't think they know about you and Jack. Not yet."

"But you're gonna tell 'em?"

"Not necessarily. Not if I can ask you some questions and I like your answers."

"What if you don't like 'em?"

"I've always liked your answers, Doc. They're colorful—even vivid."

"You sure you haven't got something tricky going?"

"Like what?"

"How the hell should I know?"

"That's just your conscience bothering you. All I want is about fifteen minutes of your time. Maybe twenty."

There was a brief pause while Doc Amber thought it over. After he made up his mind he was brisk and businesslike.

"I'll come by and pick you up at your place in fifteen minutes. We'll ride around. If you got some questions, you can ask 'em. Maybe I'll answer 'em. Then again maybe I won't."

"That's fair enough."

"Fifteen minutes," he said. "Outside." Then he hung up.

If it hadn't been for the thick pillow that he sat on, Doc Amber wouldn't have been able to see over the steering wheel of the white Lincoln Continental. As it was he still had to tip his head back and stretch his legs a little to reach the pedals, even with the front seat pulled as far forward as it would go.

He was exactly on time. When I got into the big car he didn't offer to shake hands. All he said was, "You're getting older, St. Ives."

"We all are," I said.

Amber turned left or right at every corner until we reached Wilshire Boulevard. Then he turned west. We were still going west when he said, "Well, at least there ain't no tail."

"Did you think there would be?"

"I got a paranoiac nature," he said. "In my business I got to."

"Business seems to be pretty good," I said. "The car, the suit, the Gucci's. They are Gucci's, aren't they?"

"They just look like Gucci's. If you wanta know something, they're a hell of a lot better than Gucci's. I have 'em made over in England special on account of I got such small feet."

Almost everything about Doc Amber was small and neat and compact except his hands. They were a jockey's hands—hard and lean with long, strong looking fingers. He was wearing a double-breasted flannel suit of pale grey with a vest, which you don't much see anymore, and I had the feeling that it, like his shoes, had been made in England. His shirt was a rich cream color adorned with a neat maroon bow tie. He didn't wear a hat. A hat might have mussed his hair which went back from his forehead in thick, careful waves. At his temples it had turned a silver grey, just as though he had planned it that way.

At fifty or a little past, Doc Amber was still a remarkably handsome man with a profile that should have been on a coin, with its high forehead, strong lean nose, chiseled lips, and a chin that jutted just right. Only his eyes gave any clue to what really went on inside that handsome head. They were a dark grey, almost black, and they moved around so much that some might have called them restless. I called them shifty because that's what they were.

"Well," I said as we stopped at a light. "It's been a while."

"Is that what you wanta talk about, old times?"

"Just curious. The last time I heard you were still working the widow ladies down in Miami."

"I decided to move."

"L.A.'s your territory now?"

"L.A., Vegas, La Costa—Acapulco now and then."

"How'd you get together with Jack Marsh?"

He turned to look at me. "That's it, huh? You wanta tie me in with him."

"You're already tied in with him. I just want to know how it happened."

Amber shrugged. "There was this old broad that I was working down in La Costa. She said she was fifty-five, but Christ, she was sixty-three at least. I thought she was really gone on me, you know how they are, so I moved in for a fast close. I was using the Mexican silver mine."

"Jesus," I said, "I didn't think anybody used that anymore."

"You'd be surprised. Well, you know how it goes. For a hundred thousand I'd let her in on it although I really shouldn't because I'd have to cut the Mexican general out."

"It wheezes," I said.

"I know. Well, she was all hot for it but she tips it to her brother. The brother hires Jack Marsh and that's how me and Jack met."

"He put the chill on, huh?"

"Fast," Amber said. "I'd never been chilled off anything so quick in my life. That Jack. He was one mean son of a bitch."

"Then what?"

"Well, I come back to L.A. and I'm sitting around the Polo Lounge with this mark that I'm thinking of trying to work the spud on—you know, the stolen twenty-dollar bill plates."

"The green goods racket," I said. "Sweet Christ, that's got whiskers, too."

"They all do," Amber said. "But with a little variation they're fresh as new paint. Anyway, I'm sitting in the Polo Lounge with this mark and who should waltz in but Jack Marsh. Well, I brush the mark off quick and then Jack comes over and it turns out that he was looking for me on account of he wants to do a little business."

"What kind?" I said.

Amber turned and looked at me coldly. "That's where my story ends, St. Ives. Until I hear yours."

"Mine's simple," I said. "A rare old book was stolen in Washington and I signed on as go-between to ransom it back. It didn't work out that way and I got hit on the head by Jack Marsh and he got killed and whoever was in on it with Marsh made off with the two hundred and fifty thousand bucks plus the old book and the insurance company would sort of like to get them both back, the money and the book."

This time Amber looked at me with a frown that carved a deep V into his forehead. "Me, huh? You figure it was me who went in with Marsh?"

"You were in on part of it," I said.

Amber stopped at another light on Wilshire. "Let's go get a drink," he said, "and maybe I'll tell you the rest of it. Providing, of course."

"Providing what?"

"No cops."

"All right," I said. "Providing you didn't kill too many people, no cops."

They knew Doc Amber at El Padrino bar in the Beverly-Wilshire where we decided to get a drink. The waiter addressed him by name, solicitously inquired about his health, made sure that we got a good table, and saw to it that the peanuts were fresh. He even got us a couple of drinks, a stinger for Amber and a gin and tonic for me.

"I thought you hung out at the Happy Pelican," I said.

"The Pelican's home. This is where I work. Here and the Polo Lounge and a couple of other places."

"You were all set to tell me what Jack Marsh wanted you for."

"He wanted a tin mittens to tighten up a mark for a mill's lock he had set out in Malibu." Amber grinned and I saw that his teeth were still his own and nicely cared for. "We used to talk like that, you know."

"Nobody ever talked like that," I said.

"You'd be surprised. You want me to translate?"

"Marsh wanted you to pose as an outside authority

171

to do some additional convincing on a sure scam that he was working on a mark out in Malibu. Close?"

"Perfect."

"The mark was Maude Goodwater, right?"

"Right."

"What was your job?"

"I was the representative of the prospective buyer of that book of hers, the Pliny."

"How much was your cut?"

"The book was to go for seven hundred and fifty thousand dollars. My cut was to be a finder's fee of two percent, fifteen thousand."

"What kind of spiel did you use?"

"I talked English, careful English, like I'd learned it just last week—you know what I mean?"

I nodded.

"Then on top of that I used a lot of jargon that I picked up in a hurry."

"Where?"

"Where else? The library."

"So there wasn't any buyer?"

"Just the one I made up. I made him up to be a funny old bird, a recluse, even an eccentric who couldn't stand any publicity."

"And she bought it?"

Doc Amber almost looked hurt, as though I had questioned his professional integrity, which, in a sense, I suppose I had. "Whaddya mean did she buy it?" he said. "She woulda put up the finder's fee in advance, if it hadn't been for Jack Marsh. Hell, I could've walked out of there with fifteen thou in my pocket and no questions asked."

"Sorry, Doc," I said. "I forgot how good you are."

"I sure didn't get no fifteen thou, I'll tell you."

"How much did you get?"

"Outa Marsh? Well, good old Jack Marsh was gonna pay me a grand for my afternoon's performance. The only trouble was that Jack couldn't come up with the whole grand until his own scam peeled out for him."

"So how much did you squeeze out of him?"

Doc Amber looked around the room to make sure that nobody was listening. Nobody was. He leaned toward me and whispered fiercely, "Now, goddamn it, St. Ives, you gotta swear you'll never tell nobody this."

I crossed my heart. "I swear."

"Two hundred bucks," he said bitterly and shook his head. "Two hundred lousy bucks. Can you believe it?"

"What I find hard to believe, Doc, is that you didn't try to cut yourself in somehow on the big score that Marsh was setting up. You must have known it was big."

"Did you know him? I mean did you ever do a deal with Marsh or have him come down hard on you?"

"We only met once and briefly. He just had time to half cave in the side of my head."

"Yeah, well, that's what I mean. You don't fuck with people like Jack Marsh. Not if you want to keep on walking around and talking with all your teeth. He was one mean son of a bitch."

"So he didn't tell you what he was up to?"

"Why should he?"

"And you didn't ask?"

"I knew better than that."

"So what did you guess? As I recall, you're a pretty good guesser, Doc."

"Well, there's one thing I didn't have to guess. I just knew. I mean, if you've been doing what I do for as long as I've been doing it, then you can almost smell how bad people need money. I said need, not want. Jack Marsh needed money bad. Real bad."

"You got any idea about what he needed it for?"

Amber shook his head. "I got no idea. But I am pretty sure of one other thing."

"What?"

"You say Jack Marsh was teamed up with somebody else on this book thing?"

"That's right."

"Then it's a cinch bet that whoever it was needed money just as bad as Marsh did."

"Maybe even worse," I said.

"That's right," Doc Amber said. "Maybe even worse."

──────────── SIXTEEN

I got back to the Riverside motel at eleven and I was brushing my teeth at eleven-fifteen when the phone rang. I put down my toothbrush, went into the bedroom, picked up the phone and said hello.

"That lawyer of yours. He doesn't much like to be woke up at two in the morning, which is what it is back east." The voice was a little slurred, but not too much. I didn't have any trouble recognizing it.

"How are you, Fastnaught?" I said.

"Not too bad, good buddy. Not too bad at all." .

"Sounds like you're having a party. All by yourself."

"A little celebration, St. Ives. Just a little celebration."

"What's the occasion—or is there one?"

"You know what I told you back in Washington?"

"You told me a lot of things back in Washington."

"Yeah, but the most important thing I told you was that I was gonna call you and that's what I'm doing. I called you in New York but you didn't answer."

"Shame on me."

"That's because you were out here. I mean, that's why you didn't answer in New York."

"I think I can follow that."

"So I called your lawyer in Connecticut and—" Fastnaught chuckled. "He sure as hell didn't like being got out of bed at two o'clock in the morning. That's what it is back east, you know. There's a time difference. Three hours."

"I thought it was two."

"Nah, it's three. So this lawyer of yours—Myron Greene—he's a Jew, ain't he?"

"You want me to ask him?"

"Anyway this Jew lawyer of yours, and that's what I'd get if I needed a lawyer, a smart Jew one—"

"His name used to be O'Malley, but he changed it."

"Hah, hah. Well, anyway he told me where you were out here so I thought I'd call you up and let you know, just like I promised."

"Know what?"

"I got it wrapped, St. Ives. I got it wrapped with a big blue ribbon. And tomorrow morning I'm gonna go down and see this buddy of mine in the LAPD and we're gonna get us a warrant and then we're gonna go over and make us a bust."

"Who?"

"Who what?"

I think I bit my lip. Or maybe I just ground my teeth. "Who are you going to bust?"

"Well, now, that's what I was sorta planning on telling you when you got over here."

"Over where?"

"Where I'm at. I thought you'd come over here and we'd have a couple of belts and then I'd tell you how I done it and then I'd get to see the look on your face. That's what I'm looking forward to—the look on your face."

"Incredulity mixed with awe."

"Huh?"

"Nothing. Why don't you just tell me over the phone?"

"Nah. Huh-uh. That wouldn't be any fun. That way we couldn't do any celebrating. But I'll tell you what I'll do."

"What?"

"I'll give you a hint—a big fat hint—and then by the time you get over here, if you're half as smart as you seem to think you are—maybe you'll have it all figured out just like I do. You sort of think you're a pretty smart son of a bitch, don't you, St. Ives?"

"Brilliant, really."

"Yeah, well, see how brilliant you are on this little item. Jack Marsh, that guy I shot in Washington. Well, Jack Marsh was worth a hell of a lot more dead than he was alive."

"That's it?"

Fastnaught chuckled again. "Yeah, that's it. It's a beauty, isn't it? I mean it's sort of a puzzle the way I told you, but maybe you can get it worked out by the time you get over here." He chuckled again. "But you probably won't so then we can have a couple of short ones and then I'll get to see the look on your face that I'm looking forward to seeing when I tell you all about it. Okay?"

"Sure," I said. "Fine."

"Well, I'll see you in about fifteen minutes."

"Fastnaught," I said.

"Yeah, what?"

"You forgot something."

"What?"

"You forgot to tell me where you are."

Fastnaught's motel was on La Cienega near Rose-wood Avenue. I got out the city map that the motel furnished its rooms with and looked it up. It was two miles away from where I was on La Brea. Maybe a little more. I thought about calling Guerriero but it seemed ridiculous to get him out of bed to take me someplace that was just two miles away. If I were in New York, I would have taken a cab or the subway or maybe even a bus. But this was Los Angeles where there wasn't any subway and the city buses, from what I had observed, took mysterious routes on a weekly basis. As for cabs, I might get one in fifteen minutes. Or thirty. Or maybe even an hour. There was another possibility, of course. A grim one. I could walk.

After having decided to make the sacrifice I felt that I needed something to quicken my step. I took a large jolt of Scotch right out of the bottle. I had no shame. I patted my pockets to make sure that I had the motel key, closed the door carefully behind me, and started off on what I was sure would turn out to be a fool's journey.

Actually, it wasn't too bad a walk. The temperature was pleasantly cool, the sidewalks were broad and unbroken, there were no hills, and I scooted right along

178

at what I estimated to be a steady four miles per hour. Once, a black and white patrol car slowed and its moustachioed occupants gave me a careful appraisal. I waved at them and got a curt nod in return.

Fastnaught's motel, which was called the Colony Inn, would probably be included in the same general classification that applied to mine: cheap. It was built in a deep U of cinder-block units and there was enough room left over in the middle of the U for a small swimming pool.

I started back toward the base of the U where Fastnaught's room seemed to be, from the way that the numbers ran. A car door slammed somewhere. Then an engine started and a pair of headlights came on. Somebody was leaving.

The car backed out and started down the same leg of the U that I was on. Its headlights splashed over me and I put my hand up to shield my eyes. I edged over toward the pool to get out of the car's way.

I knew something had gone wrong when the engine screamed as the driver jammed the accelerator all the way down. Then I heard the tires screech as they laid a thick layer of rubber on the cement drive. The car's headlights switched on to bright, almost blinding me, but I could still see what was going to happen next. I was going to get flattened. I backed up furiously until my heels hit something and I couldn't back any farther. There wasn't any place to go or any time to run because two tons of Detroit craftsmanship was about to slam into me and kill me so I did the only thing I could do. I fell into the pool.

I could say I dived or jumped but I didn't. I just

fell. You get just as wet that way. I came up blowing and swearing and found that I had fallen into the deep end. I swam a couple of strokes till I came to the edge and heaved myself up and over the side. I sat there on the edge of the pool and shook and waited for somebody to come up and ask why I had jumped into the pool at midnight with all of my clothes on. But nobody came. That may have been because nobody heard. Or if they did, they didn't care.

I got up and squeezed at my clothes, but it didn't do much good. Fastnaught would love this, I decided. It would give him something else to chuckle about. I started walking back toward his room, my wet shoes squishing and squashing. When I got to number twelve, I knocked. When nothing happened, I pounded on the door and yelled, "Wake up, Fastnaught!"

Somebody yelled, "Knock it off, out there!" It wasn't Fastnaught though because Fastnaught didn't have a woman's voice.

I tried the door on the chance that he had left it unlocked. Drunks do funny things. It turned easily in my hand and I went in. The lights were off and it took me a moment to find the switch. I turned them on.

His tongue bulged out of his mouth and it was beginning to blacken—or at least turn dark. His blue eyes were popped and staring. I kept waiting for them to blink, but they didn't. They would never blink again. He lay on the floor next to the bed. His legs were twisted up under him. He had on slacks and a shirt and socks. No shoes. It was probably his drinking uniform. On his left temple was a dark bloody wound—half bruise, half cut. I smelled whiskey, a lot of it. A broken whiskey bottle lay on the floor and its contents had soaked into the rug. On the table next to the bed was another bottle of whiskey, unopened, a glass that still had some ice in it, three bottles of soda, and six cigars. I looked down at Fastnaught again. There was a dark red mark around his throat where somebody had wrapped or wound something around it, a rope, a wire, or a cord, and used it to choke the life out of him.

I knelt down beside him. I had a vague idea that I should touch him somewhere to make sure that there was no life left, but I couldn't bring myself to do it although my hand got almost halfway to the dark mark on his neck.

I rose and looked around the room and wondered whether I was going to be sick. Something sour and nasty kept rising in my throat. I moved over to the writing desk. On it were a set of keys, a billfold, some change, and a clean handkerchief. I picked up the billfold and looked inside and counted the money. There was seventy-six dollars. There was also a slip of paper that looked as if it had been torn from a spiral notebook. There was a name written on the paper and a telephone number. I wrote them both down on an envelope. The name was Carl Vardaman. It didn't mean anything to me and I wondered what it had meant to Fastnaught.

I suppose the panic set in then. It must have been panic, although the wet clothes were part of it. I started shaking, almost uncontrollably. My teeth chattered. I started for the door, but stumbled, and almost fell. I caught myself on a chair. Next to the chair and the bed lay Fastnaught. For a moment I thought that he had

181

turned to watch me, but he hadn't, of course, because he was dead and there was nothing that I could do about it except say, "Goddamn it, Fastnaught, I'm sorry," although it was a couple of moments before I realized that I had said it aloud.

I called the police from a phone booth three blocks away. Then I somehow made it back to my motel, stripped off my wet clothes, turned on a hot shower and stood under it until the shaking went away and the sense of panic subsided.

After that I sat in the chair that was covered in lime green plastic and drank whiskey and got very, very drunk.

----------------- **SEVENTEEN**

The dentist kept drilling the wrong tooth. I told him that it was the wrong tooth, but he only smiled and after he was through drilling it he pulled it out with a huge pair of pliers and held it up for me to see. It made my head hurt and it hurt even worse when he reinserted the tooth into my mouth and tried to pound it back into place with a big hammer.

I woke up then and the dentist was gone but the pounding was still there, although it was someone pounding on my door. It didn't help the pain in my head which was centered just back of my eyes. It felt as if someone were stabbing at them with a piece of rusty metal.

I opened my eyes then and swung my legs over the side of the bed. I had made it to the bed, I saw, but not under the covers. I was wearing only a pair of shorts. A black wave of guilt washed over me and I shuddered. Then the nausea hit and someone pounded on the door again.

I got up and opened it. It was Guerriero. He stood there in the bright sunshine all dressed up in his glowing youth and his white smile and his nice, healthy tan. For a moment I thought of killing him, but instead I told him to come in and then asked him to excuse me because I had to go into the bathroom and throw up.

It all came up, of course. The ribs and the whiskey and the memory of the night before. I didn't look at it. I kept my eyes closed. I sat there on the bathroom floor, wrapped around the toilet, and vomited until there was nothing left. After that I got up, my eyes still tightly shut, flushed the toilet, brushed my teeth, and splashed my face with cold water.

I went back into the bedroom then and Guerriero was sitting in the lime green chair looking as though he might be thinking of whistling because he felt so well and it was such a splendid day.

I sat down on the bed and held my head in my hands. "I don't want you to say anything," I said. "I just want you to do something for me. It just possibly might save my life because I'm really quite near death."

"You look it, too," he said.

"In that pile of clothes over there is my billfold. In it is some money. I would like you to go over there and take out a generous sum. It would help if you tiptoed."

Guerriero went over and took out the billfold. "Hey," he said, "the money's all wet."

"Yes, it probably is. But maybe it will still buy what I need to save my life."

"Okay, what do you need?"

"First, go to a drugstore and get some aspirin. A lot of aspirin. Next, stop off and get me a quart of black coffee someplace with lots of sugar. Finally, find a liquor store and get a fifth of vodka and some cans of tomato juice."

"That's all? Don't you want something to eat?"

"Just go," I said. "If you're back within ten minutes, there's a slim chance that I might live. But it's highly doubtful."

An hour later it was better. The aspirin had relieved any headache. The black coffee had cut through some of the alcoholic fog. And the vodka and tomato juice were patching up my nerve ends. However, there was nothing that I could take for the guilt and remorse that gnawed at me with sharp little bites. Only time would help. A week, a month, or perhaps even a year. After that I could think of Fastnaught lying there dead on the motel room floor and of my scuttling away into the night and instead of sharp black pangs perhaps there would be only a slight involuntary shudder.

I wondered how long it would take for the Los Angeles police to tie me in with Fastnaught. Two phone calls would do it, or if they were unlucky, or tired, or even a little sloppy, it might take three. I decided that I could count on hearing from them by tomorrow or the day after at the latest. By then I might have some answers to the hard questions that they would ask. By then I might even tell them the truth.

I finished the vodka and tomato juice and put the glass on the writing table. Guerriero was sitting in the green chair watching me with a slightly amused expression.

"You're not going to die after all," he said.

"The magic elixir worked again."

"What's on for today?"

I found the envelope that I had written the name on the night before. The envelope was a little damp. "I've got a name and a phone number," I said. "I'd like to find out something about the name and then maybe I'd like to go see him."

"Maybe?"

"It depends on who the name turns out to be. If he turns out to be somebody's long lost second cousin, we can forget him."

"What's the name?"

"Carl Vardaman. One n."

Guerriero shook his head. "You don't want to see him."

"I don't?"

"I heard about him when I was working in Vegas. They call him Carl the Collector."

"Is that where he is, Vegas?"

"Sometimes. But most of the time he's here in L.A. If somebody gets in over a hundred thousand or so and can't pay, they turn him over to Vardaman. I heard a lot of stories about his collection methods. Nasty stories mostly."

"Broken legs, arms, things like that?"

Guerriero shook his head again. "That's old stuff. Vardaman's methods are more refined. The first thing he does is make whoever he's trying to collect from take out a life insurance policy for twice as much as they owe in Vegas. Vardaman sometimes even advances the first quarterly premium. The beneficiary, of course, is Vardaman. From what I understand, the realization that you're worth more dead than alive is a hell of an incentive to go out and scratch up the money. So far, I've never heard of Vardaman collecting on any of the policies. But he probably will one of these days—just for the publicity value."

"What else does he do—or does he?" I said.

"He's a speculator, from what I hear. Land, gold, commodities, anything that's fast and profitable. I think he's got an office in Beverly Hills someplace. Carl Vardaman Enterprises."

I took the telephone book out of the writing desk and looked under the V's. Vardaman's office was on Wilshire Boulevard. I wrote the address down and handed it to Guerriero. "Let's go," I said.

Guerriero shook his head. "You certainly run with a funny crowd," he said.

"I'm in a funny business."

Vardaman's office was on the ninth floor of one of those black glass office buildings on Wilshire just before it runs into Santa Monica Boulevard. The name on the dark wood door said Carl Vardaman Enterprises. It didn't say walk in, but I did anyhow.

A woman of about thirty with long black hair looked up from the desk where she was working on a crossword puzzle. She looked me over with large blue eyes that had dark circles under them. Then she gave me a bored half smile and said, "May I help you?"

"I need to see Vardaman," I said.

"Do you have an appointment?"

"No. I just found out about it."

Some of her boredom went away. I might be a puzzle. She seemed to like puzzles. "About what?"

"The mixup."

187

She frowned. "We could go on like this all day. What mixup?"

I sighed. I made it a long, heavy one, full of exasperation. "The mixup in the Marsh policy. You do know about the policy, don't you—on Jack Marsh?"

It was all I had to go on and I wasn't at all sure where it would lead, if anywhere. She frowned again. "I thought that was all—" She stopped. "Have you got a name?"

"St. Ives," I said. "Philip St. Ives."

"And you're with—"

I didn't finish her sentence for her the way that she seemed to want me to. I smiled at her instead. I tried to make it warm and friendly and even engaging.

"I think you'd better tell him I'm here."

She frowned again and picked up the phone. "A Philip St. Ives is here," she said. "He says it's something to do with a policy on Jack Marsh." She listened for a moment and then said, "Yes . . . yes . . . I see. All right." Then she hung up the phone and looked at me again. "If you'd like to wait, Mr. Vardaman will see you in a few minutes."

"Fine," I said and sat down in a chrome and leather chair and took out a cigarette. I smoked that one and then I smoked another one. The brunette kept busy with her crossword puzzle. Twice, she resorted to a paperback dictionary for help. Nobody came and nobody left. The phone didn't ring. Carl Vardaman Enterprises seemed to be having a slow day.

I was debating about whether to light a third cigarette when the inner door opened and a man came out and stood there looking at me with the expression of someone who has just discovered ants in the sugar.

He wasn't particularly tall, yet he was thick—all of him. He stared at me and then he frowned and the frown made deep horizontal wrinkles across his tanned forehead.

"You," he said, "smart-ass. In here." He jerked a thumb over his shoulder and disappeared through the door. I got up and started after him.

"Is that Vardaman?" I said to the brunette.

"Himself," she said.

On the other side of the door that Vardaman had gone through was a short carpeted hall with three other doors leading off of it. I went through the door that was open. Vardaman was standing behind his desk next to a high-backed swivel chair.

"Close the door," he said.

I went back and closed the door.

"Sit down."

I sat down.

"I don't know what you know about me," he said.

"Very little."

"Let me talk, will you. When I want you to talk, I'll tell you. It took me two calls to find out all I want to know about you. That's all. Two calls. One to Vegas, then one to New York. Just two calls and I got your whole life history. You're very small beans, aren't you?"

"Very small," I said.

He sat down in his chair and moved a piece of paper on his desk. His hands were thick and covered with dark hair that ran from the backs of his fingers up to the heavy wrists that were exposed where the sleeves of his brown suede shirt jacket had been carefully turned back just once. Underneath the jacket he wore a pale tan shirt with a long collar. It was open not only at the throat but also halfway down his chest where another patch of dark hair grew.

There was more dark hair on the top of his head and at the sides and also down his neck. It had a carefully tousled look that must have cost him at least a quarter of an hour a day. Beneath the hair was a hard, handsome face with black eyes that glittered, a mouth that sneered easily and often, and a big chin with a jutting ledge that I could have laid a dime on.

He leaned back in his chair and worked on me with his black eyes. Although he seemed to search for a while he apparently found nothing about me to like. I was just the morning nuisance and he wasn't going to let it spoil his lunch.

"There are two ways I could handle this," he said after he tired of his staring game. "One would involve doctors, bone specialists probably, and a long rest in the hospital. That would be kind of—" He searched for a word. "Sordid, wouldn't it?"

"Sordid," I said.

"The other way—well, I don't much like the other way either because it means that anybody with a long nose like yours can come around sticking it into my private business where it hasn't got any right to be stuck. You follow me?"

"Closely."

"You know, you're the second guy this week that's stuck his nose into my private business. Yesterday, it was some Washington cop. Today, it's some New York grifter. Where's it all going to end?"

"One wonders," I said.

"Now I run a business here and I've got to run it efficiently or else I'm gonna be out on the street nickel-

and-diming it and scratching around to make a living, which from what I understand is sort of what you do, isn't it?"

"I couldn't have described it better myself."

"So what I'm gonna do, smart-ass, is I'm gonna tell you exactly the same thing I told that Washington cop yesterday, no more, no less."

"What could be fairer."

"Okay. Here goes. Mr. Jack Marsh was in debt to a client of mine who runs a perfectly legal business in Las Vegas. Mr. Marsh owed my client one hundred and twenty-five thousand dollars. My client turned the matter over to me for collection. I talked with Mr. Marsh who fully acknowledged his debt but asked for an extension of time. I said okay. We both agreed that because we live in an uncertain world it would be wise if Mr. Marsh took out a life insurance policy in the amount of two hundred and fifty thousand dollars with Carl Vardaman Enterprises as the beneficiary. This was done. Before Mr. Marsh could pay off his debt he got himself killed in Washington, D. C., and I got fifteen witnesses, smart-ass, who will put me in Vegas at the time that Marsh was getting himself shot. That's it."

Vardaman rose. I rose with him. "Just one question and I'll be on my way."

"You'll be on your way anyhow."

"Who did Marsh take out the insurance policy with?"

"Pacifica Life and Casualty. He said he had a buddy over there but I don't remember the guy's name and I don't wanta look it up."

"Spivey," I said. "Max Spivey."

EIGHTEEN

The afternoon Hearst paper gave Fastnaught a good ride on its front page with the headline:

WASHINGTON COP FOUND
SLAIN IN L.A. MOTEL

The headline almost had more facts than the story itself, which went on to say that an anonymous phone call had led police to the discovery of the body at the Colony Inn motel shortly before midnight yesterday. The story had Fastnaught's name and rank right, but it had his age wrong. He wasn't forty-seven. He just looked that way.

I read all about Fastnaught over a martini and an omelet that I had ordered for lunch at a place on La Cienega that Guerriero had suggested after I told him that I was buying. When I was through reading about

Fastnaught I put the paper down and went back to my martini.

"How'd you like Vardaman?" Guerriero said. Since I was buying, Guerriero was having a steak and a beer.

"I was glad I didn't owe him any money," I said. "Is he as nasty as he says he is?"

"Nastier. Was he any help in whatever it is that you're trying to do?"

"I'm not sure," I said. "After lunch I think I'll go back to the motel and lie down and think about it."

"Then what?"

"I'll think about that, too."

The phone rang at three o'clock. I was lying down so I sat up, picked up the phone on its second ring, and said hello.

"St. Ives?"

"That's right."

"You still want to get that book back?"

It was the same voice, the one that was too high to be a man's and too low to be a woman's and again it was talking around something, a coin in the mouth, a finger, or maybe even a couple of marbles.

"You're supposed to be dead," I said.

"You mean you thought this was Jack Marsh's voice?"

"I did up until now."

"You thought wrong. I'll ask again. Do you want to get that book back?"

"Let's hear your proposition."

"One hundred thousand. The same kind of bills as before and no cops this time."

"That wasn't my idea."

"Well?"

"I'll have to check with the insurance company."

"You've got two hours," the voice said. "I'll call you back at exactly five o'clock."

The phone went dead and I hung it back up. I sat there on the edge of the bed and thought for a moment. The Pliny book was insured for $500,000. The insurance company had already parted with $250,000. To keep from parting with the full half million it might be willing to part with yet another $100,000. But it wasn't my decision so I picked up the phone and called Max Spivey at Pacifica Life and Casualty.

When Spivey came on I said, "I just got a call from what sounded like that same voice that I talked to in Washington. Whoever it is said that you can buy the book back for one hundred thousand. You haven't got much time to make up your mind."

There was a silence. Finally, Spivey said, "I'm thinking."

"I don't blame you."

"I can't make a decision like that on my own. Can you get over here?"

"Fifteen minutes," I said.

Guerriero had gone for gas, but he was back in ten minutes. The Pacifica Life and Casualty Company building was about five minutes away on Wilshire and by the time I got to Spivey's office I was only five minutes late.

It was the first time I had ever seen Spivey behind a desk and although it was a large one he seemed to dwarf it. He had his coat off and his shirt sleeves rolled up and he looked very much like a hard-working business executive who just happened to be twice as big as everybody else.

"We're going in to see Ronnie at three-thirty."

I thought back for a moment. "Ronnie Saperstein, isn't it?" I said. "He's the guy, the ex-agent, who started all your tits and ass stuff."

"We like to think of him as chairman of the board. So does Ronnie."

Spivey leaned back in his chair and ran a hand through his hair. "I called the police this morning after I read about that Washington cop. Fastnaught. I thought I might fill them in on what he was working on. They already knew. He'd checked in with them as soon as he got out here. But they sent a couple of detectives over to talk to me anyhow. This whole thing is turning into a real mess."

"Did you tell them about me?" I said.

He nodded. "Any reason I shouldn't have?"

"No."

"Have you turned up anything?"

I shook my head. "Not much. I did learn that Marsh was in hock to some gambling types in Vegas for about a hundred and twenty-five thousand. The name Vardaman mean anything to you? Carl Vardaman?"

Spivey leaned forward toward me. "It means one hell of a lot to me. It means a quarter of a million dollars to the company. He's the business associate who's the beneficiary on a policy that Jack took out with us."

"Is that what Marsh told you?"

"He said he had gone in on a business deal with Vardaman."

"Did he say what kind?"

Spivey thought about it. "It was some kind of land speculation. They had optioned a big chunk of land down near San Diego. Marsh said each of them was going to take out a policy naming the other as beneficiary just in case. It seemed legitimate enough. It's done all the time."

"There wasn't any land deal," I said. "Vardaman is a collector for some gambling types in Vegas. If whoever he's trying to collect from is a slow pay, he makes them take out life insurance for twice as much as they owe. When you know that you're worth twice as much dead as alive it concentrates the mind wonderfully, as I think Dr. Johnson once said. Or something like it."

I could almost see Spivey's mind working. "Marsh had somebody in on it with him. If this Vardaman—"

I cut him off. "Vardaman says he can come up with fifteen witnesses who can place him in Vegas at the time that Marsh got shot. He couldn't fix that many people."

Some of the excitement drained out of Spivey's face. He leaned back in his chair. "We're right back where we were. Which is exactly no place."

"Not quite," I said. "You might still get the book back."

"But we're still out—" The phone on Spivey's desk rang. He picked it up, said hello, listened, and then said, "We'll be right down." He hung up and looked at me. "That was Ronnie. Let's go."

We went down a hall and then into a large corner

office that was paneled and carpeted and furnished to look exactly like what an ex-Hollywood agent might think that the office of the chairman of the board of a prosperous insurance company should look like.

A short, wiry man with a lot of pure white hair bounced up from behind a big carved desk. "You're the hotshot," he said, moving around the desk and holding out his hand. "I'm Ronnie Saperstein."

We shook hands and he moved back a little and cocked his head to one side while he examined me with dark eyes that flickered in a tan face that was just beginning to grow a lot of lines. "I was wondering what you'd look like," he said. "When people are in a funny business, you sort of expect them to look funny. But most of the time they don't. For example, you don't. You look like the second lead."

"The one who doesn't get the girl," I said.

"Or the book," Saperstein said. "But I hear we've got a second chance. Let's sit down over here and run through it."

We sat down on a couch and a couple of easy chairs that were drawn up around a low coffee table. Saperstein crossed his legs. "You got a call," he said. "Tell me about it."

"It was the same voice that I dealt with in Washington. It could be a man; it could be a woman. Whoever it is said they'd sell the book back for one hundred thousand dollars."

Saperstein looked at Spivey. "What do you think, Max?"

"We're already out two hundred and fifty grand."

"But we're going to be out five hundred grand unless we get that book back. What the hell did we ever start insuring crap like that for anyhow? We should have stayed with tits. Nobody ever stole a pair of tits."

"Not yet," Spivey said.

Saperstein looked at me. "What about you, St. Ives? You think whoever called is on the level or do you think they're just making noises?"

I shrugged. "It was the same voice. I'd say there's a chance."

"Good chance or poor chance?"

"Just a chance," I said.

"Maybe we should turn it all over to the cops," Spivey said.

Saperstein thought about it. "We turn it over to the cops and what does it get us? The book? Doubtful. The two hundred and fifty thousand we're already out? Equally doubtful. Whoever we're dealing with must be expecting cops. They're probably going to come up with all sorts of conditions that're going to make cops impossible anyway. Isn't that the way these things usually work, St. Ives?"

"Usually," I said.

He looked at Spivey. "How much time have we got?"

"Till five, isn't it?" Spivey said and looked at me.

I nodded. "That's right. Whoever called me is going to call back at five."

Saperstein uncrossed his legs and slapped his palms on his knees. "All right," he said. "I say go. What's your end of it, St. Ives, ten percent?"

I nodded. "That's my usual rate. But what would it be worth to you if I got the book back along with whoever's got it and whatever's left of the two hundred and fifty thousand dollars that got lost in Washington?"

Spivey stared at me, a look of curiosity on his face. Saperstein was grinning. "You'd cross the thief?" he said.

I shook my head. "The thief was Jack Marsh. Marsh is dead. We're dealing with whoever was in on it with Marsh. But you asked me if I'd cross him. Or her. My answer is yes, if the money's right."

I could almost see Saperstein's mind clicking off some figures. "What would you say to seventy-five thousand—if you wrap it all up like you said."

"That's an offer?" I said.

"It's an offer. What do you say?"

"Put it in writing," I said.

────────────── NINETEEN

Max Spivey brought the $100,000 by my motel at twenty minutes to five and we counted it together.

"You must know some bank vice-president," I said.

"We know a lot of bank vice-presidents, but none of them likes to part with a hundred thousand in cash, especially at four in the afternoon."

"Well, it's all there," I said and closed the cheap black attaché case that Spivey had placed on the bed. "Would you like a drink?"

"I wouldn't mind."

I opened a fresh bottle of Scotch that I had bought earlier and mixed two drinks. Spivey took a big swallow of his and leaned back in the lime green plastic chair. The chair creaked.

"Did you ever double-cross anybody like this before?" he said.

I shook my head. "Never. It's not good for business."

"But since they crossed you back in Washington, you figure it's okay if you cross them this time, right?"

"If you want to go into the morality of it, I guess that's the way it is."

"How're you going to do it?"

"I don't know yet," I said. "It depends upon what kind of a switch they come up with. All I need is a good look at whoever it is that I turn the money over to. When the thief sets up the mechanics of a switch, there's usually a moment when he's got to depend on the go-between's not peeking. Well, I'm going to peek."

"What if they come up with something so clever that you can't?"

"Then I'll have to do something else."

"What?"

"I don't know yet."

"You want to know something?" Spivey said.

"Sure."

"I think you earn your money."

We sat there in a not uncomfortable silence with our drinks until five o'clock. At two past five the phone still hadn't rung. "You think they're going to call?" Spivey said.

"They said they would."

It rang at three minutes past five. I picked it up on its second ring and said, "Yes?"

"Do you have the money?" the distorted voice said.

"Yes."

"Okay, I'm going to say this just once so I want you to listen real good. First, get yourself some real heavy fishing line, about thirty or thirty-five feet of it. Second, have the money in something that you can tie the fishing line to. Third, go to the Santa Monica pier at two fifty-five. That's two fifty-five A.M. Start walking toward the end of the pier. Take your time and go real slow because we're going to be watching. Go along the pier until you come to the bar and grill called Moby's Dock. It's on the left. When you pass Moby's Dock start counting your paces. Ninety-nine paces past Moby's Dock there's a place where the pier sort of juts out. That's where you lower the fishing line over. We'll tie the book to it and you can draw it up. Then you tie what you've got the money in to the fishing line and lower that. Wait three minutes while we check the money. After that, you can take off. But don't try anything tricky because there's going to be somebody between you and where the pier starts and if you try something tricky, you won't make it back to New York. You got it?"

"I've got it," I said.

The phone went dead. I hung it up and turned toward Spivey. "The Santa Monica pier at three A.M." I said. "I lower a fishing line over the end and bring up the book. Then I lower the money. It's nice."

"Where does that leave you?" he said.

"You mean how am I going to be able to cross them?"

"Uh-huh."

"I don't know yet. I probably won't know until I'm in the middle of it."

"What if you can't?"

"Well, if I can't, I can't. And then you'll be out another hundred thousand, but you'll have the book back, and I won't make as much money as I'd hoped I would."

"One other thing," Spivey said.

"What?"

"What if they decide to cross you again?"

"That thought occurred to me."

"And?"

"If they try a cross, I'll put contingency plan number two-A into operation."

"What's that?"

"I don't know yet," I said.

Guerriero didn't show up until six o'clock. He came in carrying a brown paper sack.

"Did you get it?" I said.

He nodded. "I had to go see a couple of people, but I got it." He handed me the paper sack. I opened the sack and took out a .38 Colt. It looked like a Detective Special. I made sure that it was loaded and then put it on the bedside table.

"Well, what did you decide?" I said.

"Tell me again how much," he said. "That's the only part that I like so far."

"Five thousand dollars," I said.

"That's a lot of money."

"It is indeed."

"It would pay for a year's tuition."

"It would pay for a lot of things. Well?"

"I've been trying to rationalize it."

"And?"

"Well, I think I've come up with something."

"What?"

"If I did it and you paid me five thousand, and I spent it on tuition, then I'd sort of be working my way through college, wouldn't I?"

"Sure you would," I said.

I rented a car from the Hertz people. I rented a big Ford LTD because I have this theory that before long all that they will be renting are Honda Civics, and that by renting a big Ford I was actually doing research into what will soon become the nation's past.

The Ford had power everything and after Guerriero dropped me off at the Hertz place I drove around a while, running the windows up and down, adjusting the seat, and playing with the button that locked the doors. The Ford also had a lot of scat to it and on a quiet street where there didn't seem to be any kids or cops I jammed the accelerator down to the floor. The Ford took off with a whoosh and by the time I had reached the end of the block I was doing an effortless seventy.

Back at the motel I found Maude Goodwater's number and dialed it. When she answered on the third ring, I said, "This is Philip St. Ives. You mentioned that we might have dinner sometime. I was wondering if you could make it tonight?"

"Well, I'm not quite sure—"

"There's been a new ransom demand for the book and the insurance company has agreed to pay it. In fact, there's a chance that I might get the book back tonight, but I have to eat first. Why don't you join me?"

There was a silence. Finally she said, "It's—well, it's such a surprise, I mean about the book, I don't know quite what to say."

"Say you'll have dinner with me."

"I'd already decided to do that. The reason I said I wasn't sure is because I meant I wasn't sure what I could feed you."

"I was sort of planning on us going out."

"I wouldn't hear of it," she said. "When I mentioned something about dinner, I meant dinner here. Do you like lamb chops?"

"Very much."

"Lamb chops it'll be. Seven or seven-thirty?"

"Fine."

"I'm dying to hear about the book, but I'll make myself wait until you get here. My God, I'm excited! I didn't realize I was so caught up in this thing."

"I haven't got it back yet."

"Don't tell me any more. You can tell me all about it when you get here."

"Okay," I said. "It'll be about seven-thirty."

We said good-bye and I hung up the phone and found the L.A. map and studied it until I was pretty sure that I could get to the Santa Monica pier without getting lost. I reached under the pillow and took out the .38 and put it in my jacket pocket. I picked up the cheap attaché case and glanced around the room to see if there was anything that I had forgotten. There didn't seem to be so I went out to the Ford and locked the attaché case in the trunk.

I took Wilshire out to San Vicente and followed that until I found a hardware store. I went in and bought a length of fishing line and a flashlight. Next door was a liquor store so, remembering my manners, I bought a bottle of red wine and, a couple of doors down, a bunch of flowers.

Back in the Ford, I headed west on San Vicente. Under the coral trees that grew along the strip that divided the boulevard, some serious-faced joggers, hard breathers all, plugged along in their slow and solitary race toward better health.

When San Vicente ended at Ocean Avenue I turned left and drove until I came to Colorado Avenue. I turned right and went up over a viaduct that had a 10 m.p.h. sign on it. On the other side of the viaduct was the broad Santa Monica pier that seemed to stretch a half a mile or so out into the ocean.

On the pier I drove slowly past the old merry-go-round, which seemed strangely familiar to me until I remembered that it was the one that had been used in *The Sting,* although the film was supposedly laid in Chicago. Past the merry-go-round on the pier's left-hand side was a series of hamburger and hot dog stands, a shooting gallery, some souvenir shops, a fishmonger, and maybe a double handful of strollers, mostly young, who wandered up and down in search of amusement.

When I got to Moby's Dock, which turned out to be a modest looking restaurant and bar, I stopped the car next to a No Parking sign and got out. I crossed the pier and, starting at the west edge of Moby's Dock, began walking toward the end of the pier, counting my paces. When I got to ninety-nine I stopped.

The pier's grey metal railing jutted out in a shallow U-shape to form a railed-in area. It was about wide enough and deep enough for four people to stand in. An elderly black man was standing in it, a fishing pole in his hand, a look of patience on his face.

I moved up next to the black man and peered over

the railing. The sea, a soiled grey, lapped at the wooden pilings about thirty feet below. As I turned to go the black man nodded to me. "Catch anything?" I said.

"Just fishin'," he said and grinned. I grinned back and returned to the Ford. I drove on down the pier until it ended at a group of small buildings that housed a bait shop and the pier's maintenance office. There was a turn-around place that I used, and started driving slowly back toward the beginning of the pier.

When I got to the railed-in enclosure that jutted out from the edge of the pier, the old black man was putting some fresh bait on his hook. He looked up and saw me and gave me a wry smile. I waved at him and drove on, looking carefully at all the nooks and crannies and doorways and recesses that, once it grew dark, somebody could hide in. There were a lot of them.

I left the pier thinking that I didn't much like what I had seen. I didn't like it because it had no emergency exit. There was only one way on and one way off and there were too many places that somebody with a gun or a knife or just a very large rock could hide. From the point of view of whoever had the stolen book the pier was perfect. From my point of view it was awful.

From Ocean Avenue I cut down to the Pacific Coast Highway and headed toward Malibu. It was almost seven o'clock and I got to drive into a sunset that had to be called spectacular, for lack of a better word. It had bands of hot reds and angry oranges and at its center was the glowing yellow ball of the sun that seemed to be plunging into a crimson sea.

The sun had almost gone down by the time I reached Maude Goodwater's house on Malibu Road. I took the gun from my jacket pocket and locked it in the glove compartment. Carrying the flowers and the bottle of wine I went around to the trunk and took out the attaché case.

She opened the door to my ring and accepted the wine and the flowers gracefully, as if they were a complete surprise. She was wearing a long, loose gown of a thin creamy material that was gathered at her waist with a golden cord. As she arranged the flowers in a vase I watched her body move beneath the dress. I found it an extremely erotic sight.

"What would you call it?" she said, turning to watch the sun as it dropped down behind two low hills of a point of land that edged out into the sea.

"I was thinking of 'spectacular' on the way out," I said. "But that's not really a very good word."

"It's different every night," she said. "Sometimes it's so beautiful that the only way I can react to it is to sit down and cry. That's sort of dumb, isn't it?"

"No," I said. "Not really. Funny, but I thought that the sun was supposed to set in the west. Isn't that west?" I pointed at the ocean.

She shook her head. "That's south. The coast curves out here and the house faces due south. It mixes everybody up."

"You'll miss it, won't you?" I said. "The beach and the house and the sea. I know I would."

She nodded slowly, as if she were trying to decide just how much she would miss it. "I'm really hooked on it and it's got so that it's hard to imagine living anywhere else. Maybe if I get the book back, I can sell that and maybe stay on for a while longer. Do you think I really will get it back?"

"I think so," I said. "After I pay them the hundred thousand tonight, or this morning, I guess, they'll have milked it for all that it's worth."

"Let's have a drink," she said, "and then you can tell me about it. What would you like, a martini?"

"I'd like a martini, but I think I'd better have Scotch."

She went over to the bar and came back after a minute or two with the drinks. She handed me mine and then sank gracefully onto the couch. I joined her.

"They called at three o'clock this afternoon," I said. "I say 'they' because I have to assume that there's still more than one person involved. Anyway, it's the same voice that I talked to in Washington. It's so distorted that it's hard to tell whether it belongs to a man or a woman. Whoever it belongs to offered to sell the book back for a hundred thousand dollars. I checked with Max Spivey and his boss at the insurance company, Ronnie Saperstein. They agreed to pay it. The switch will take place at three o'clock this morning on the Santa Monica pier. That's about it."

She nodded thoughtfully and then took a sip of her drink. "The insurance company is going to be out an awful lot of money, isn't it?"

"Three hundred and fifty thousand."

"But I'll get the book back? I mean, if I sell it, they won't get part of that, will they?"

"No. It's insured for five hundred thousand. That's what they'd have to pay you, if they didn't get it back.

This way they'll only have to pay three hundred and fifty thousand."

"They must not be very happy," she said.

"They're realists," I said. "Unhappy realists, I suppose."

She leaned back on the couch and looked at me. The thin white material of her dress pressed against the nipples of her breasts, outlining them perfectly. I stared at them for a moment. Then I reached out and touched the one that was closest to me. She looked down at my hand.

"It's hard, isn't it?" she said.

"Yes," I said. "It is."

"How does it make you feel?" she said.

"Excited."

She took my hand and moved it to her other breast. I caressed the nipple with my fingers. "I don't mean this," she said. "I mean how do you feel about doing what you're going to have to do?"

"Excited," I said. "Nervous, maybe."

She ran her tongue over her upper lip. "Is there a chance that something might happen?"

"Yes."

She pressed my hand harder against her breast. I could feel her heart beating. "Tell me what might happen," she said, her breathing fast and shallow. "Tell me what they might do to you, even if you have to make it up."

So I put down my drink and told her. And as I told her my hand went from her breast to the smoothness of her thighs. I kept on talking because it seemed to be what she wanted—or needed. I was next to her now, her body pressed tightly against mine, my fingers moving deep into her wet warmness. Her head was back, her mouth open, and her tongue seemed to be tasting the things that I told her.

There was a quick, frantic period as we stripped off our clothes and then she was down on her knees in front of me and her mouth and tongue were doing incredible things and I quit talking because there really wasn't anything left to say and besides, she wanted to talk. She didn't really talk, of course. She made strange little cries and once she moaned from far down in her throat. And then she was on the couch and I was over her and then I went inside her and her mouth opened wide, as if she were going to scream, but she didn't. The frenzy mounted as we lunged at each other and she started making those strange little cries again, interrupting them to whisper, "Hurt me, hurt me a little, please." So I hurt her a little, but not very much, and she screamed this time, and then there was one more long series of frantic lunges and counter-lunges that led us up to the silent explosion, which was what it was all about.

We lay there on the couch breathing at each other for a while and then she said, "I sometimes think I'm a little weird, don't you?"

"No."

"I mean all that talking stuff. That's weird."

"Does it help?"

"It turns me on. God, how I hate that phrase."

"Then don't use it."

"It excites me, the talking I mean. It's sort of s-m, isn't it?"

"Sort of, but it's harmless."

"Do you like it?"

"What?"

"Hurting me like that?"

"I like pleasing you and if that's what you like, then I'm all for it."

"And you don't think I'm too kinky?"

"Not enough to count."

She sat up and handed me a cigarette, taking one for herself. "When this is all over, what will you do, go back to New York?"

"Yes."

"Are you married? Or did I ask that?"

"You didn't ask, but I'm not."

"But you were, weren't you? I can tell."

"How?"

"Guys that haven't been married don't fuck as well as you do."

"Thank you very much."

"Really. There're little things that they just don't know about."

I sat up. "I didn't know that."

"It's true. How often do you do this?"

"I suppose as often as I can."

"I don't mean screwing. I mean this go-between thing."

"Oh. That. Several times a year. Two or three. Maybe four sometimes. That's several."

"What do you do in between the go-between stuff?"

"Not much. I sort of mess around. I read a lot. It's one of the few things that I do really well so I do a lot of it. I'm a very good page turner."

212

"You could do that almost anywhere, couldn't you?"

"I suppose."

"Why don't you do it here?"

"You mean in L.A.?"

"You know what I mean. I mean here—on the beach. With me."

"You're not talking about marriage, are you?"

"You know I'm not talking about that. I like you. I think I'd like living with you for a while. You seem to like the beach and the ocean. You even seem to like me. So why don't we like each other together for a while? It'll probably be six months before I have to give up this place. After that, if it's working, maybe we can find another place down the road. Or maybe we'll just move on—separately. What do you think?"

I smiled. "I think it's an interesting idea."

"That's not a yes or a no. It's not even a maybe."

"What it is," I said, "is a 'this is so sudden.' "

"You mean you'd like to think about it?"

"Uh-huh, I'd like to think about it."

"You're not hung up on this male aggressiveness thing, are you?" she said. "I mean, it doesn't bother you that I did the asking?"

"Not in the least," I said. "It happens all the time."

Later, after the lamb chops, and the wine, and more lovemaking, which turned out to be far more gentle and less frantic than the first time, I got quietly up from the large bed, picked up my clothes, and moved into the living room. I had left Maude Goodwater asleep, her mouth slightly open, her breathing deep and regular.

I put on my clothes, found the Scotch, poured myself a drink, and stood by the big glass windows looking out at the dark ocean. The tide seemed to be coming in and the big waves rolled over and slapped themselves down on the sand and then hissed as they slid back into the sea. I liked the sound that the sea made and I wondered why I had never lived beside it in the past. I considered the invitation that I had to live beside it. It was really more of a proposition than an invitation and it was the second one that I had received within a week. I looked at my watch and saw that it was one-fifteen. That meant it was four-fifteen in New York and I wondered if Mary Frances Ogletree, the gambler-doctor, was sleeping as deeply as Maude Goodwater was.

I thought about my two invitations to share bed and board and decided that it was the times and not my winning ways that had prompted them. The times were indeed changing and I suppose I was changing along with them, but not quite quickly enough. The problem was that although I would indeed like to move in with Maude Goodwater and share her Malibu beach, I would also like to move in with Dr. Mary Frances Ogletree and let her teach me how to play no-lose five-card stud.

Both invitations had been, as far as I could tell, sincere and well-meaning and prompted by good intentions, which, as everyone knows, pave the way to hell. And no doubt each woman thought that I would be nice to have around the house, probably not much more bother than a well-mannered cat. My back would be nice and warm against their feet at night and during the day I could provide a giggle or two and once or twice or perhaps three times a year I could go out and do something clever to get back something that had been stolen and thus earn a whole bunch of money that would enable me to come up with my half of the rent and the grocery bill.

It would be a very adult arrangement, but spiced with a bit of wickedness because of my occasional consorting with thieves, and there would probably be nothing but jolly times until the day came, as I know it must come, when my nerve went.

It may not be this year, or next year, or even the year after that, but one of these nights when I'm all dressed up in my Southwick suit, my pebble-grained loafers, my regimental striped tie, and my airline flight bag stuffed with a couple of hundred thousand dollars or so, I'll be walking down a black alley toward its center where the dark danger lies and I'll stop, and stare, and turn around, and go back toward where the lights are. After that I will no longer be what I am now, which is a go-between. I will not be less than I am now, I will simply be something else. I'm not sure what. Older, I suspect.

And so because of this and although I protested it, a certain amount of pride, I knew that I would not move in and play house with either woman. I was flattered, but not flattered so much that I could pretend that it wouldn't end badly. I didn't even want to think about how it might end because I had gone through all that once before and once should be enough for any sensible man.

So I stopped thinking about that and started thinking about what I would have to do at three o'clock that morning, which is when I would start earning my money. I was thinking very hard about it and I didn't hear her until she said, "What time is it?"

I looked at my watch. "Two o'clock."

"Have you been up long?"

"No. Not long."

"What're you thinking about?"

"About what I'm going to do."

"You mean about us?"

"I've been thinking about that, too, but right now I'm thinking about what I'm going to have to do at three o'clock."

"Are you scared?"

"A little."

"Are you always scared?"

"Yes."

"Can I do anything for you?"

"No."

"I'd be scared," she said, "having to go out and do what you do without even knowing who's going to be out there waiting for you."

"It's not quite like that this time," I said.

"Why?"

"I know who's going to be out there waiting for me."

—————————————————— TWENTY

It started to rain at 2:25 A.M., just before I left. Maude Goodwater went to a closet, rummaged around, and brought out a tan raincoat. She held it out to me.

"It belonged to him," she said.

"Jack Marsh?"

She nodded. I took the raincoat and slipped it on. It was a little big, but not enough to bother about.

"Well," I said. "I'm off." I pulled her close to me and kissed her.

"Call me," she said. "Call me as soon as it's over."

"All right."

I went out to the Ford and got in. I took the flashlight and the .38 from the glove compartment and slipped them into the raincoat's pocket. I made sure that I had the fishing line. After that I started the car and drove east on Malibu Road until I got to the Pacific Coast Highway.

There was almost no traffic on the highway. The rain

fell steadily, a hard, soaking April rain that would make things green. The windshield wipers ticked and tocked back and forth and I kept the Ford at the speed limit, a steady 45 miles per hour.

It took twenty minutes to reach Santa Monica. I took a ramp-like road up to Ocean Avenue and turned right. Everyone seemed to have gone to bed in Santa Monica. From what I had seen of the place, they probably had been there for several hours.

I drove slowly, checking my rear-view mirror. There was no one behind me. At five minutes until three I parked the Ford not far from the Colorado Avenue entrance to the Santa Monica pier. I got out and went around to the trunk, unlocked it, and took out the cheap attaché case.

The rain still fell steadily as I turned up the collar of the coat that had belonged to the late Jack Marsh, shifted the attaché case to my left hand, wrapped my right one around the butt of the .38 in the raincoat pocket, and started walking.

I walked over the viaduct that led to the pier. A row of lights, like street lamps, lined each side of the pier and shined weakly through the steady rain. The pier, as far as I could tell, was deserted.

I walked slowly through the rain, swiveling my head on my neck, trying to see into the dark recesses that were formed by the hot dog stands and the shooting gallery and the souvenir stand and the pinball emporium. All I saw were a lot of wet, dark places that could hide anything from a small thief to a large elephant.

I passed Moby's Dock and kept on walking. When I

218

reached the place where the pier poked out over the ocean I stopped and looked around. All that I could see was a lot of rain. I took the heavy fishing line from my pocket and looked at my watch. It was one minute until three. I counted slowly to sixty, tied one end of the fishing line around a white handkerchief, and then lowered it over the side of the pier. I kept on lowering it until I felt a tug. From the way that the line jerked I thought I could feel someone tying something to the other end of the line. Finally, there was another hard jerk and I started hauling the line back up. There was something on the end of it, something that weighed at least forty pounds.

I hauled the line all the way up. It was tied around a heavy green plastic garbage bag. I untied the line and used the flashlight to look inside the bag. Inside was the Pliny. I bent down and tied the line around the handle of the cheap attaché case, and started lowering the case over the side. When there was another sharp tug, I stopped lowering it.

I waited a moment, leaned over the metal railing, and switched the flashlight on. A white face looked up at me through the rain. The white face belonged to someone who was crouched over in a small boat. A skiff. Next to the crouching someone was the open attaché case. The money was being counted. It was also getting rained on. The mouth in the white face opened as if it wanted to say something, but I switched off the flashlight, and started hurrying away toward the entrance to the pier. I had seen enough. I had recognized the white face. It had belonged to a woman and the woman was Virginia Neighbors who had once been secretary and a little more, perhaps a lot more, to the late Jack Marsh.

I had peeked when I shouldn't have and now I knew for certain who else had been in on the theft of the Pliny with Jack Marsh. It was interesting information and I wanted to get to a phone and tell the police all about where they might find Virginia Neighbors and one hundred thousand dollars in ransom money.

I hurried along the pier, the green garbage bag containing the Pliny in my left hand, my right hand still in the raincoat pocket, wrapped around the butt of the .38 revolver. The rain was falling harder now and it seemed colder as it trickled down the back of my neck.

He stepped out of the rain and the shadows and said, "That's far enough."

I stopped. I stopped because of the gun that he held in his big hand. The big hand belonged to Max Spivey. He moved toward me slowly and stretched out his left hand, the one that wasn't busy with the gun.

"I'll take the book," he said.

"It's not worth much stolen," I said.

"By tomorrow it won't be stolen."

"How're you going to explain me?"

"You got shot and whoever shot you got away with the money after they turned over the book."

"She made the calls, didn't she, all those calls with the funny deep voice?"

"Virginia? Yeah, she made them. With direct dialing you can make all sorts of calls. The book, St. Ives. Just hand it over real slow."

I moved my left hand back just a bit and then brought it quickly forward in an underhand pitch. I released the garbage bag and it sailed toward Spivey, if forty pounds of book can sail. It wasn't a hard pitch and Spivey had plenty of time to duck. He ducked down and to the right and pulled the trigger of his pistol and there was that bang and then a kind of a thunk and the garbage bag fell at his feet. In trying to shoot me, Spivey had shot the book instead.

I had no time left so I shot Max Spivey through Jack Marsh's raincoat pocket. The bullet slammed into his left leg and he stumbled, but he didn't go down. He pointed his pistol at me again so I decided to shoot him again. I tried to aim at his left leg, but I'm not a very good shot. The second bullet must have gone into his stomach because he dropped his pistol and clutched at his middle and then went down on his knees and looked up at me with shock and a lot of disbelief.

"The gun," he said. "Jesus, it hurts. The gun. I wasn't counting on you for a gun."

"No, I guess not," I said and knelt down beside him.

"You said in Washington—you said you wouldn't shoot anybody over money."

"I must have lied," I said.

Max Spivey looked at me and his mouth worked as if he wanted to say something else. Instead he fell over on his side and drew his legs up and screamed. He kept on screaming as I got up and trotted off into the rain.

At the end of the pier I found a telephone booth and called the police. Then I went down some steps that led to the beach. I walked out on the wet sand toward the ocean. The small boat was drawn up on the sand and two figures were standing by it. One of the figures was dressed all in black. It was Johnny Guerriero in a wet suit. The other figure was Virginia Neighbors. She was standing by the boat, wearing a dark raincoat, and clutching the attaché case.

"How'd it go?" I said to Guerriero.

"Just like you said. When I popped up alongside the boat and pointed the gun at her she almost fainted."

"You son of a bitch," Virginia Neighbors said. I wasn't sure whether she was talking to Guerriero or me.

"We heard some shots," Guerriero said.

"That was me."

"Was it Spivey?" Virginia Neighbors said. "Did you shoot Spivey?"

"Yes," I said. "I didn't want to, but there wasn't much choice."

She stared at me and the rain that streaked her face failed to conceal the bitterness. "He said you wouldn't use a gun. He said you told him in Washington that you wouldn't use a gun."

"I'll have to tell you what I told him," I said.

"What?"

"I lied."

I reached out and took the attaché case from Virginia Neighbors. "Let's go," I said. I turned and started back toward the beginning of the pier. In the distance I could hear Max Spivey screaming. He kept on screaming until the ambulance came and took him away.

─────────────── TWENTY-ONE

The chili was dripping all over the detective-lieutenant's fingers and he was trying to wipe them off with the wax paper and he was making a mess of it.

"The best goddamned hamburgers in town," he said, "and for napkins they serve wax paper."

"They are good," I said, taking another bite of mine.

The detective-lieutenant was Mason Patrika and he had been a friend of Fastnaught's. I had spent the entire morning, four very unpleasant hours, with the Los Angeles police and at one o'clock Patrika had appeared and offered to buy me the best hamburger in Los Angeles. We were sitting in his car at a drive-in type place called Tommy's on Beverly Boulevard. We were eating hamburgers and drinking Cokes and Patrika was telling me what the police had found out about Max Spivey.

"We didn't get anything out of him, you know," he said.

"So I understand."

"He screamed and screamed all the way to the hospital and just when he got there he stopped screaming and died. But the woman, what's her name, Neighbors, yeah, Virginia Neighbors, well, she talked and for all I know, she's still talking. She said Fastnaught got out here and started digging in pretty good, I mean he was getting close and so Spivey called him and set up a meeting and when Spivey got there, he picked up a bottle of booze and cracked old Fastnaught over the head with it and then used a piece of wire to choke him with, but you say you knew that."

"It had to be Spivey," I said. "But I didn't know who it was at the time."

"Well, they picked up a print from underneath where you flush the toilet. It was Spivey's. After he got through choking Fastnaught he must have used the john to piss or maybe throw up in. Who knows? Sometimes they do that, you know, throw up."

"Whose idea was it?" I said.

"You mean the whole schmear?"

"Yes."

"It was Spivey's. He needed money. I mean, he really needed it bad. He had gone into a couple of deals, land deals, and they'd gone sour. Well, he knew Jack Marsh was always up to his ears in debt so he approached him— laid it all out for him, according to the Neighbors woman. Marsh jumped at it. He paid the little guy, what's his name?"

"Doc Amber."

"Yeah, Amber. He paid him a few bucks to go and make a spiel to Maude Goodwater about how he had a buyer for the book. She fell for it and then when Marsh got to Washington he just picked up the book from the Library and then disappeared. The Neighbors woman was in Washington with him when she made all those calls."

"What'd she use?" I said.

"What do you mean?"

"To distort her voice."

"Oh. A couple of nickels, she said. She just put a couple of nickels in her mouth and then talked as deep as she could. Then in Washington it was Max Spivey who drove off with the money and the book after Fastnaught shot Marsh."

"His hair was wet," I said.

"Whose?"

"Spivey's. When I finally got back to the hotel, his hair was wet. Or damp."

"He could have taken a shower."

"Or been out in the snow."

"Or that," he said. "What else? I mean, you say you knew it was Spivey even before you went out to make the buy-back last night."

"I thought it was him," I said. "I was pretty sure it was him. It was something he said."   •

"When?"

"When we were in his boss' office. The woman had called me and told me that I had until five o'clock to decide whether the insurance company would spend· another hundred grand to buy the book back. When his boss asked how much time they had, Spivey said until five o'clock. I hadn't told him that."

"Gee, it was a real clue, wasn't it?" Patrika said, not bothering to keep the sarcasm out of his voice.

"Sure."

"Why didn't you do something about it?"

"Such as? You mean you think I should've called the cops and said, hey, this guy Spivey already knows that we have until just five o'clock to make up our minds. I didn't tell him that, so why don't you come down and get him and toss him in the jug? Something like that maybe?"

"It wasn't much, was it?"

"Hardly anything."

Patrika took the last bite of his hamburger, looked at his messy fingers, and sighed. "In my rear pocket," he said. "There's a handkerchief."

I reached into his rear pocket and took out a fresh white handkerchief. He wiped his fingers on it. "I oughta keep some Kleenex in the car," he said. "My wife gets mad as hell when I get chili all over my handkerchiefs." He looked at me. "How come you didn't get any on your fingers?"

"I'm naturally neat," I said.

"Fastnaught," Patrika said. "You know, he was a pretty good cop."

"I know."

"But he was drinking. A lot of cops drink too much. It's sort of the cop's disease."

"And doctors and lawyers and writers and painters and traveling salesmen."

"Yeah, I guess you're right. I guess we all try to be a little special, don't we? I mean, we all think if we didn't have such rough jobs we wouldn't drink so much. But still, Fastnaught must have been getting pretty close to get himself killed."

"He was working the insurance angle," I said. "He found out that Jack Marsh was in hock to some people in Vegas and that he'd taken out a policy with Spivey's company that made the collector the beneficiary. That smelled and that's probably all that Fastnaught needed."

"To get himself killed, you mean."

"That's right. To get himself killed."

* * *

226

Guerriero pulled up in front of the house on Malibu Road and cut the engine. "Will you be long?"

"Not long," I said. "How much time do we have?"

"It's about forty-five minutes to the airport."

"We've got a little more than an hour then."

I got out of the van and went through the wooden gate and across the patio and down the three steps. I rang the bell and Maude Goodwater opened the door. She smiled and I smiled back. I followed her into the living room.

"Would you like a drink?" she said.

"No, I don't think so."

"Well, it's over, isn't it?"

"Yes, it's over. I'm sorry about the book."

"I wasn't talking about that. I mean it's over between us."

"It didn't really get started, did it?"

She smiled again, this time a sad, almost wistful sort of a smile. "It might have worked out."

"You would've had to put up with more than you bargained for."

"What does that mean?"

"I'm not sure," I said.

She turned and looked out at the ocean. It was a pale blue dotted with frosty looking whitecaps. "Funny," she said. "It seems I might be able to stay here after all. I got a call a while ago."

"From whom?"

"From a man who'd heard about the book—about it's having a bullet hole through it. He wants to buy it. He offered me six hundred thousand. I didn't think he was for real so I had my lawyer call him. He's what we talked about—rich and eccentric."

"He collects books with bullet holes through them?"

"He collects things that are connected with violence. Expensive things."

"Well, I'm very happy for you."

"You sure you won't change your mind and play on the beach with me?"

"I'm tempted."

"But not enough."

"Not enough to cause you more trouble than you've already had."

"You wouldn't be any trouble."

"You'd be surprised," I said.

Guerriero switched the van over into a faster lane on the Santa Monica freeway. He looked at me and then looked back at the road. "You mind if I ask you kind of a personal question?"

"No, I don't mind."

"How much will you make off of this thing out here?"

"About seventy-five thousand, less expenses. The expenses will run about six, I guess, counting your five thousand."

"And how long did it take?"

"About a week in all. Maybe a little more."

"Let me ask you another real dumb question."

"All right."

"When I go back to school, is there anything I might study that would help me become a go-between?"

"Like me?"

"Yeah. Like you."

I thought about it for a while. "Ethics," I said finally. "You might study ethics."

THE PERENNIAL LIBRARY MYSTERY SERIES

Ted Allbeury

THE OTHER SIDE OF SILENCE	P 669, $2.84
PALOMINO BLONDE	P 670, $2.84
SNOWBALL	P 671, $2.84

Delano Ames

CORPSE DIPLOMATIQUE	P 637, $2.84
FOR OLD CRIME'S SAKE	P 629, $2.84
MURDER, MAESTRO, PLEASE	P 630, $2.84
SHE SHALL HAVE MURDER	P 638, $2.84

E. C. Bentley

TRENT'S LAST CASE	P 440, $2.50
TRENT'S OWN CASE	P 516, $2.25

Andrew Bergman

THE BIG KISS-OFF OF 1944	P 673, $2.84
HOLLYWOOD AND LEVINE	P 674, $2.84

Gavin Black

A DRAGON FOR CHRISTMAS	P 473, $1.95
THE EYES AROUND ME	P 485, $1.95
YOU WANT TO DIE, JOHNNY?	P 472, $1.95

Nicholas Blake

THE CORPSE IN THE SNOWMAN	P 427, $1.95
END OF CHAPTER	P 397, $1.95
HEAD OF A TRAVELER	P 398, $2.25
MINUTE FOR MURDER	P 419, $1.95
THE MORNING AFTER DEATH	P 520, $1.95
A PENKNIFE IN MY HEART	P 521, $2.25

THE PRIVATE WOUND	P 531, $2.25
A QUESTION OF PROOF	P 494, $1.95
THE SAD VARIETY	P 495, $2.25
THERE'S TROUBLE BREWING	P 569, $3.37
THOU SHELL OF DEATH	P 428, $1.95
THE WIDOW'S CRUISE	P 399, $2.25

Oliver Bleeck

THE BRASS GO-BETWEEN	P 645, $2.84
THE PROCANE CHRONICLE	P 647, $2.84
PROTOCOL FOR A KIDNAPPING	P 646, $2.84

John & Emery Bonett

A BANNER FOR PEGASUS	P 554, $2.40
DEAD LION	P 563, $2.40
THE SOUND OF MURDER	P 642, $2.84

Christianna Brand

| GREEN FOR DANGER | P 551, $2.50 |
| TOUR DE FORCE | P 572, $2.40 |

James Byrom

| OR BE HE DEAD | P 585, $2.84 |

Henry Calvin

| IT'S DIFFERENT ABROAD | P 640, $2.84 |

Marjorie Carleton

| VANISHED | P 559, $2.40 |

George Harmon Coxe

| MURDER WITH PICTURES | P 527, $2.25 |

Edmund Crispin

| BURIED FOR PLEASURE | P 506, $2.50 |

Lionel Davidson

THE MENORAH MEN	P 592, $2.84
NIGHT OF WENCESLAS	P 595, $2.84
THE ROSE OF TIBET	P 593, $2.84

D. M. Devine

MY BROTHER'S KILLER	P 558, $2.40

Kenneth Fearing

THE BIG CLOCK	P 500, $1.95

Andrew Garve

THE ASHES OF LODA	P 430, $1.50
THE CUCKOO LINE AFFAIR	P 451, $1.95
A HERO FOR LEANDA	P 429, $1.50
MURDER THROUGH THE LOOKING GLASS	P 449, $1.95
NO TEARS FOR HILDA	P 441, $1.95
THE RIDDLE OF SAMSON	P 450, $1.95

Michael Gilbert

BLOOD AND JUDGMENT	P 446, $1.95
THE BODY OF A GIRL	P 459, $1.95
FEAR TO TREAD	P 458, $1.95

Joe Gores

HAMMETT	P 631, $2.84

C. W. Grafton

BEYOND A REASONABLE DOUBT	P 519, $1.95
THE RAT BEGAN TO GNAW THE ROPE	P 639, $2.84

Edward Grierson

THE SECOND MAN	P 528, $2.25